Lost Without Her

Lost Without Her

POURNIMA NAVANI

Srishti
PUBLISHERS & DISTRIBUTORS

Srishti Publishers & Distributors
Registered Office: N-16, C.R. Park
New Delhi – 110 019
Corporate Office: 212A, Peacock Lane
Shahpur Jat, New Delhi – 110 049
editorial@srishtipublishers.com

First published by
Srishti Publishers & Distributors in 2018

10 9 8 7 6 5 4 3 2 1

This is a work of fiction. The characters, places, organisations and events described in this book are either a work of the author's imagination or have been used fictitiously. Any resemblance to people, living or dead, places, events, communities or organisations is purely coincidental.

Printed and bound in India

This book is dedicated to my father, Mr Nand Ishwar Navani.

Thank you Papa for bringing me my first comics at four and my first mystery book when I was a teen. You introduced me to the wonderful world of written words and inculcated in me the ritual of reading every day.

Physically you may not be by my side, but I know you are with me each step of the way.

Love you always.

Acknowledgements

Writing this book was a happenstance. I always made notes and wrote down story ideas, but never thought I would actually ever complete one, much less have it published.

My mother, Mrs Madhumati Navani, had faith in my storytelling abilities and pushed me to complete this one. Thank you Maa, you are my strength.

Also, she was of the mind that this story needed to be told to showcase the extremes of child sexual abuse and the extent of trauma almost every other child in India and around the world goes through. Unfortunately, some victims don't survive.

My sisters, my best friends, Sonal and Swati, thank you for reading and rereading every word I emailed, inspite of your busy schedules, and always coming back with critical, helpful and most honest feedback.

Shri Purshottam Navani, thank you for being the voice of my conscience, always.

Mr Arun Kumar Dalmia, my mentor, my guide, a father figure in my life after my papa, thank you sir for always showing me the correct path.

Shrinivas Balasubramanian, the subject of a Biography that I am writing, thank you for being my harshest critique and one of my most wonderful friends.

Vatsal Desai, you are the best friend everyone deserves and I am blessed to have.

Thank you Herumb Khot, you are the first person I narrated this book to and are the man who encouraged me whenever I had doubts.

Advocate Shri Vinod Gangwal ji, thank you for taking out time from your hectic schedule to help me whenever I had a query.

Stuti, my editor, I actually cannot thank you enough for spending hours talking to me and guiding me each step of the way and correcting my mistakes, on paper and otherwise.

And last but not the least, thank you Mr Arup Bose, Mr Arjun Ghosh, and Srishti Publishers, for believing in me. I couldn't have asked for a better platform for my first book.

Somewhere in Tamil Nadu, about equidistant from Chennai, Coimbatore and Tiruchirappalli, lies the town of Marsti, quite hidden, undiscovered. Roughly, the thousand or so tourists that visit here a year don't bring much revenue, but the small population of about twenty-five hundred residents likes it that way.

The town on this late Saturday afternoon, as on most days, was quiet and peaceful.

The school had let off for the week at 1.00 p.m. and the watchman, an old man with a walking stick lying across his feet, was dozing on the chair by the gate.

The only mall in town, which didn't have a theatre or any expensive stores, with fans and lights switched off, was closed too.

The Tamil Nadu State Transport Corporation provided the single means of public transport in the way of an hourly bus service in the morning and evening. The next bus would start at 5.30, so the ticket checker and bus driver were snoozing inside the bus. There were three autorickshaws lined up next to the bus station; their drivers enjoying their afternoon siesta.

In a small one-man run barbershop, sat a group of men chatting about the last town meeting where the town mayor had reprimanded local bar owner, David D'mello, for indulging drug traffickers. The barber, a middle-aged man from central India, who sometimes smoked a joint or two himself, thought the mayor was being too harsh.

"*Penkal marrum araciyal!*" (Women and politics!) he said with discontent, about Mrs Madhu Krishnan, the town mayor's dislike for David. "They always get too emotional about such things," he continued as he rubbed the tobacco in his palms.

Marsti, with most people tucked away inside their respective one storey and two storeyed houses, and apart from some street dogs and a one in half-hour rickshaw passing somewhere, lay somnolent, itself.

Apart from a lone figure,waiting with diminishing patience, sitting stock still on the footpath, ducked behind a huge peepal tree, across the street from Inspector Anthony George's two storeyed house, observing it.

Julie, a seventeen-year-old girl with pale complexion and long auburn hair, wearing skinny jeans and a tank top, could be seen through the huge French windows fixing lunch in the kitchen.

She had received a call, spoken excitedly into her mobile, and then spent the next ten minutes rummaging into her school bag. Finally pulling out a pair of shorts from her bag, she had rushed into the bathroom.

Face hidden underneath a black hooded jacket, and wearing loose faded black jeans, the bulky person waited, careful not to draw any attention, hoping, almost sure but not quite, that the call had been from Julie's boyfriend Peter.

After another thirty minutes, just as the figure was getting restless and was about to get up, the thumping sound of a

Royal Enfield was heard and a thunderbird drove into sight. Renewed energy coursed through the spectator's body.

A tall lanky boy astride a bullet, which had seen better days, was riding down the road. He parked his bike some distance away and walked towards Anthony's house.

For this hiding person, the wait was finally over. Jubilant, a sly smile curved the lips.

The boy, with a college backpack on his shoulder, his complexion darkened by unhealthy habits, face almost invisible under untidy, greasy hair, with pants almost falling off his butt, swaggered towards the house. He took his phone out of his back pocket.

"Hello, open the door," he slurred into the phone with an unknown accent.

Inside the house, Julie was nodding her head with the phone pressed against her ear. She ushered the little Samantha out of the backdoor with her water bottle and a plate of sandwiches and hurried back to open the front door.

As soon as the boy entered the house and the main door closed behind him in a hurry, and the curtains were drawn.

Two silhouettes could be seen walking upstairs to Sam's bedroom through the drapes.

The person finally got up from behind the tree with a wince, having sat in the same position for the last two hours.

There were only three houses on this lane, each surrounded by woods on three sides and fenced against dogs and other animals. No one fenced against robbers or killers because those kinds of things were unheard of in Marsti.

Walking slowly, with a hunched back and hands in pockets, down the deserted road, past Tony's house, the only person who could have seen this stranger was Amanda. She stayed diagonally opposite from Tony's house, but she had already had her lunch and had retired to her bedroom.

Her house, schedule, and habits had been as keenly observed by this stranger, as were Anthony and Sam's, and Tony's next door neighbours, Mr and Mrs Ananth.

Walking a little ahead of where the fence of Tony's property ended, the stranger stopped and looked around.

The road was still deserted. The person stepped off the cement asphalt and started following the muddy trail that led inside the woods; a small detour lead to Anthony's backyard.

Samantha, Tony's six-year-old daughter, was picking flowers from the rose and jasmine plants, plucking them carefully, collecting these in the front panel of her frock.

The figure walked towards the child confidently now, assured knowing Sam's room – where Julie was with her boyfriend – overlooked the front of the house. "I am going to give you a treat now, Sam. Ready or not, here I come!" The last words were spoken loudly, with enthusiasm, for Sam to hear. The stranger walked through the small wooden back gate of Tony's house.

At the sound, Sam looked up at her father's friend and a surprised smile played on her face, showing the gap at the front of her teeth where she had recently lost a couple.

"Hi!" chirped Sam.

"Hey Sammy, how are you? Wanna play?"

"I can't play right now. I have so much to do before Dada comes home," said the child lisping a little.

"What do you have to do, princess?" asked the bulky figure, brushing a hand up Sam's arms and liking it when Sam shrugged her shoulder and shuddered at the touch, unknowingly.

Laughing shyly at being called a princess, Sam said in her sweetest and most grown up voice, "I have to decorate the house for Dada, then I have to make a bou.. bouq... *malar puccentu*," she finally said in her mother tongue and continued, "then I have to do my homework, help Dada prepare dinner, learn the new poem, read Casper to Dada. So much to do!" finished Sam, now looking at her just arrived friend importantly.

"Oh! But these flowers are not as pretty as the ones I just saw back there."

"Really? Where?" Sam queried excitedly, interested in the conversation now and trying to peer in the woods. "I want the best flowers for Dada; you know he loves flowers. My mommy did too."

"I would get them for you princess, but you might not like my choice of colours."

"Are they in many colours?"

"Oh yes! All the colours of rainbow. Do you know how many colours there are in the rainbow?"

"Yes!" Sam jumped up, dropping the flowers in the process.

"There are seven colours, but violet is my favourite and Dada says I look best in it!" she said looking down at her lavender dress.

"You do, darling!"

"Can you take me there to collect the flowers, please?" asked Sam innocently. "I will make a bou.. bouquet for you too!" she finished proudly at finally pronouncing the big word.

"Of course. Come with me!"

"Wait, I have to tell Julie. Dada says I shouldn't go anywhere alone."

"You are not alone, I am with you, and we will surprise Julie with a bouquet too."

"No! She is not very nice to me when Dada is not around. She pinches me when I ask her anything and once when I told Dada, she lied and he didn't believe me. I don't like her," Sam said softly, sounding almost guilty for outing her nanny.

"Then we don't have to tell her anything. Come!"

"Oh..." Sam stood thinking if her Dada would be upset about her going into the woods. "I am not alone, and you are Dada's friend, and mine. Let's go!" decided the six-year-old excitedly.

Her friend held out a hand that Sam took smiling. "Dada will be so happy!" said Sam. "Do they smell nice too?"

"Oh, yes! They are fragrant just like you, princess," said her hooded friend picking up Sam's small figure, taking a deep breath into her neck, lips almost on her skin exhaling, and started to walk briskly. Sam giggled.

As Samantha Anthony George crossed her house's backyard gate and started to where the flowers were waiting to be plucked, all she could think of was how pleased her Dada was going to be.

As the bell rang to indicate the end of the last period of school, children in a sea of dark blue pants and pleated light blue skirts, with light blue shirts and red ties, hastily packed their bags and rushed out of their classrooms.

Keith Morgan, the history teacher, was in no hurry. His class room slowly emptied of fourth standard children wishing him good afternoon and good day. He packed the home work books on his desk at leisure. Dressed in paisley shirt, black pants, and brown loafers, unshaved beard, specs with big rims stood on his nose, he sat there, long after everyone had left. One hand laid lazily on the desk, a small smile played on his face. While his other hand rubbed his crotch, hidden from prying or innocent eyes, under his un-tucked shirt and stomach hanging almost over his thighs. With the smile widening, he sighed, got up, and walked down the corridor towards the boy's toilet.

Walking in, he opened every toilet cubicle to make sure it was empty. He locked the door from inside slowly and put his bag on the wash basin platform, and then the forty-year-old carefully climbed the same platform. He reached up and from behind the old tube light removed the battery pack attached to a small screw bolted in one of the tube light holders.

He had ordered this set sometime back, and it had been easy enough to install it, just remove one screw and replace it with fake screw which was a camera; no one suspected something they couldn't see.

The battery pack lasted six hours and that was just enough recording to last him a week.

As he was getting down, he heard someone turning the doorknob and then there was a hard knock on the toilet door. "Who is inside? Open the door! You are not allowed to lock the toilet from inside!" finished Dinanath, the school janitor, sounding angry.

"Dinanath, it's me, Keith sir. Wait a minute," he replied hurrying down, and stuffing the camera and battery in his handbag.

"Oh! Okay sir. I have to clean the toilets. Thought it was some student. Will you be long?"

Opening the door with a smile, "No, I am done. The staffroom toilet was occupied, so used this one. Had to lock the door, doesn't look nice if a child walked in while I was using the urinal. I am their teacher, after all."

"That's okay sir," said Dinanath with a smile, and walked in carrying a bucket with mop. Such a thoughtful, well-behaved, moral teacher is Keith sir, thought old Dinanath as he looked back to see Keith Morgan walking away. In his three years at the school, he had never seen Keith sir beating a student and he was always so respectful towards the school peons, janitors, cooks, and other junior staff, unlike some other teachers. Smiling, and humming a Tamil song, Dinanath started the cleaning process.

10th September 2016
Saturday, 11.00 p.m.

"Tony, I have divided the groups into four," Arvind said putting Marsti's map on the hood of Tony's jeep, "Mr Ananth will start from behind your house, David knows the woods best around his guesthouse, and luckily, he was partially sober tonight, but I have put Leslie with him, just in case, to search in the west. Father Ranganathan will start from the north and Krishnan ma'am is going to lead the east, starting from mall road," said Arvind, standing tall, but still awkward about his height since childhood as he towered over Tony who was 6'1". In his khaki uniform, trying to sound strong, sub-inspector Arvind was trying his best not to look as terrified as he felt.

Nodding his head was all Anthony George could manage. Being the senior inspector of Marsti Police Station, he should have handled a situation like this better, but he was incapable of any coherent judgments or helpful suggestions at the moment. His mind was filled with chaotic thoughts of the worst happening to his daughter Samantha.

When Tony had reached home, Julie, Sam's nanny, had been crying. She told him that she hadn't seen Sam since 6.00 p.m. and that she was just about to call him after looking everywhere. Tony had been mad at Julie, but more than mad, he had been worried that Sammy might have walked into the woods again.

He had sent a crying Julie home with the warning that if anything happened to his daughter, she would be in trouble. Tony had run towards the woods.

There were wild animals and snakes and rats and god knows what in the woods! "Sammy, I am going to punish you this time! Why would you not understand baby! The woods are dangerous, I told you that. Oh Sammy!" Tony started yelling even before he was out the back door.

He had been searching the woods himself for the last three hours, and when he was hoarse from shouting and blinded by tears, he had called Arvind. At around 10 p.m., Arvind had called Mrs Krishnan, the Mayor and she had immediately put together a search party with the help of Arvind and her own secretary.

There were close to fifty people in the search team and more would be joining as they got calls from Mrs Krishnan's secretary.

12th September
Monday, Early morning

"Hey! Shhhh! Did you hear that?"

"What?"

"I thought I heard someone running."

"Sunil, you are high!" laughed Chris.

"I am serious. I thought I heard someone running."

"You are just hearing things! Its 5.00 a.m. Who could be running in the woods," Winston, in the process of lighting a Gold Flake cigarette, stopped short. What he was saying left hanging in the atmosphere, he removed his glasses unconsciously, slowly. He had just heard steps running in his direction and so had Chris.

With finger on his lips to quieten them, Sunil, the short, chubby guy got up from under the tree they usually came to smoke some hash or weed or do coke.

The steps were running towards them but they were hidden well between trees at the back and front and tall weed. No one came this deep into the woods at this hour.

A figure came in running about ten feet away. As the boys ducked further down, the leaves rustled, and the figure paused, slowly looking around where they were hiding. Sunil, Chris and Winston didn't move for the fear of being noticed. The figure started walking again, slowly at first, then jogging and finally running towards mall road.

Ten minutes had passed since they heard the footfalls of the hooded one. They slowly got up and looked at each other.

"Who could that have been?" Chris and Sunil spoke at once.

"Whoever it was could be up to no good," Winston said.

"Was it another druggie?"

"...or a cop?" Chris added to Sunil's question

"..Was it a ghost?"

"Come on Sunil! You don't believe in all that, do you? We have been coming here for over a year now! And since when do ghosts wear hoodies, jeans and military shoes?" Chris asked and Sunil, incredulous, looked at his feet.

"Let's leave. I think I am just sleepy."

"I need another joint to take me through tonight and tomorrow!"

"That was the last one Winston and the stash is at the guesthouse."

"Oh, come on! Just one last one. You guys have lost your high too. It's Monday and the princy has called my dad to school to complain about the fight I got into last week. I need it guys. Do it for your brother!"

"Alright," said Chris and they walked the short distance and were at David's rundown guesthouse in fifteen minutes. It was still partially furnished; the good stuff had been robbed long ago and the furniture that was left was old and dusty and mostly broken.

The school kids were told that it was haunted to keep them away. This place had been used in the beginning by horny teens, drug addicts, drunkards, and thieves, since the town council shut it down over six years ago. All sort of riff raff had made this their hangout place. It had seen some of the best parties after it had been forcibly shut down, but then Tony had heard about it after a party had turned violent and two boys had ended up breaking each other's nose and teeth, respectively. Tony had told David to hire a night watchman and that had deterred the crowd, but two years back the watchman had disappeared.

Now David's guesthouse only saw Sunil, Chris, Winston, and some adventurous out of towners once in a while.

"Sunil, get the stash! Let's smoke up here on the porch. Looks like it's going to rain."

"Winsty, you wanted a joint! You go and get it."

Winston, who had just posted his posterior on the broken but useable lounge chair, got up and went inside.

"Hey! There is someone inside, let's get out of here!" he came back immediately, scared out of his wits.

"Who!?"

"I didn't wait around to see. Let's go!"

They had climbed down the five short stairs when Chris halted and looked back.

"Guys, what if someone has found our stash?" he asked his friends, worried.

"Who would search for it behind that heavy chest?"

"Winsty, what did you see?" Chris asked doubtfully, hands on hips.

"Nothing, I didn't see anything, it was dark inside and before my eyes could adjust, I heard something. I couldn't make out what it was... I don't know! It was coming from the first floor, as if someone was scratching something... like someone crawling on the floor and then I heard a thud. And then I ran out."

"Let's leave Chris, even if someone has found our stash, we can't take the risk. With that man in the woods and now this, I am scared. Call me chicken, but I am shit scared right now," Sunil said.

Winston and Sunil pulled Chris by the hand as he started to go back towards the huge house.

Chris looked back one last time and decided Sunil had a point and let his friends pull him into a jog and then a run till they reached the road. While running, their own footsteps sounded too loud and as they went ahead with each step, the sound seemed to come from behind, as if someone was running to catch up with them right in their footsteps.

They looked back from the asphalt road, and breathing heavily spoke over each other,

"We will come back..."

"... after school today..."

"...and check the guesthouse."

"... I just want to go home..."

"...and sleep."

"Okay, after school, but we come together. No one goes alone," Sunil said.

They each looked at the woods one last time for a beat, and then at each other and parted without saying bye as the sky started to turn ashy, rainy gray with mornings first light.

13th September
Tuesday, 11 a.m.

A group of college students found Sam's body while trekking. They called the police station. Upon reaching the spot with Arvind, Tony saw his daughter – bloody and lifeless.

14th September
Wednesday afternoon

"Has the autopsy report come?"

"No sir. Shall I call the hospital and check?"

"Yes Leslie, please call and check. I need the reports," said Tony, trying to control his raising voice.

Hurriedly, Leslie picked up the phone receiver, put it on her ear, without realizing the wires were tangled and the water glass on the table was balancing on the cord. The glass spilled water on the table. Leslie got up in a hurry, almost falling herself. She started to reach for the tissue box and her hand brushed against the coffee mug, making it drop on the floor.

"Sorry sir," she said, looking scared. "I... I will make the call, sir." Leslie picked up the phone and the glass which had fallen on the desk rolled dangerously towards the edge of her desk. Her desk and the floor now strewn with papers, glass and cup shards with coffee and water on the desk and the front of her dress, she looked close to tears.

"Leslie, clean up and try to be calm. Please!"

"Yes sir, sorry sir," she managed to murmur.

With an exhausted sigh, he walked to Arvind's table, "Call the hospital, get me the reports, and I want to talk to Dr Moore and Sumanth, ASAP," Tony said exasperated, and taking the panchnama from Arvind's hands, walked towards his cabin slowly.

Arvind picked up the phone and dialled the hospital, while looking at his boss dragging his feet.

"The customer you have called is busy on another call, please try again later," heard Arvind after the dial tone.

Arvind dialled again for the Nth time since morning and got the same auto recording.

He dialled a mobile number now, instead of the landline, and it thankfully rang, but there was no answer. The mobile was picked up as he tried for the third time. Just as he was about to hang up, "Hello? Arvind, I can't talk now!" said a voice hurriedly.

"Hello! Eleena, don't hang up! Is Doctor Moore there?"

"She hasn't come yet Arvind, I have to go, there's..."

Arvind cut her, "Where is she? You know this is an emergency. The phone is constantly busy. What kind of hospital are you guys running there?" Arvind yelled into the phone.

"It has been an emergency here since morning, Arvind! So don't tell me about emergencies. I have been calling Dr Moore since morning myself. She was supposed to be in the OPD at 7 a.m. A child came in with a broken wrist last evening, four cracks in one single bone. I sent the reports to her email, she said he might require a surgery today and to have him admitted and not to give him any water after midnight. It's two in the afternoon now and the child is thirsty. Dr Moore is not reachable. Her mother is accusing me of purposely putting her child through this pain. I have been dealing with angry parents since morning, so don't tell me about emergencies." Eleena finished, finally taking a long breath after the monologue and feeling better after venting. "When she gets here, I will tell her you had called. Bye," she said and hung up.

Arvind looked at the phone as if the phone had slapped him across his face. He dialled again, "Hello?" came a voice after the second ring. "Calm down Eleena..." said Arvind in a soothing and calm, but firm voice.

"Sorry Arvind, it's been a crazy morning, and I have a headache and a stomach ache to add to it."

"Eleena, I am sorry to hear that, but baby you know why it is important that I speak to Dr Moore. When did you speak to her last?"

"Yes, I know," came the reply soberly now. "I spoke to her last night before leaving for home around nine. She told me she will be in at 6.30 to check the child's reports for surgery and then attend her OPD.

"You know, she is usually very punctual. In the last three years, she hasn't taken a single leave. I don't know where she is!" she said in panic.

"Don't worry, it must be her brother. I will swing by her house if she doesn't call by evening. Is Dr Sumanth there? I need the autopsy report and Tony sir needs to talk to him."

"I will check with Dr Sumanth. I thought he had already sent the reports. I will ask him to call you."

Before anything else, she asked again, "Arvind, is Tony okay?"

"No," Arvind replied curtly and Eleena understood. She had been devastated enough to consider suicide when her daughter had gone missing in Madurai a few years back.

Eleena's husband had been supportive and caring throughout the worst, but their marriage had broken down eventually. They had gotten divorced on mutual consent a year later, and she had moved to Marsti for a quiet life away from the memories of a lost child and a broken marriage.

"Pick me up after work? Eight?"

"I will, if I leave on time. Call you around seven in the evening, El. Love you."

"Bye."

Arvind called Dr Sumanth's mobile number and it was picked immediately. Dr Sumanth spoke before Arvind could say hello, "Tony, I was just about to call you! I have just mailed the postmortem report to your email address, please check and confirm that you have received it and I will come and meet you. This is worse than it looks. I haven't slept all night just thinking about this horror. I will come and talk to you personally. Are you okay, Tony?" he enquired with concern.

"Arvind here, Doctor, and yes, please come to the station. I just checked the mail and have received the report, but Tony sir wants to see you. When can you come?"

The old doctor breathed a sigh of relief at being told it wasn't Tony on the line. The short, frail looking man, bald save for patches of hair around his ears wiped his hand down his shirt, like wiping out something unpleasant. His brown, big eyes looked sad and were red from the sleepless night filled with nightmarish images of Sam. His hands were shaking like leaves in the wind. Dr Sumanth had been pacing the room endlessly since reaching the hospital and finding out that Dr Moore hadn't come in.

"I will leave now, should be there in half an hour. Arvind how is Tony?" he asked.

"He is as well as one can be, Doctor."

"Her body will be released today. Has Tony spoken to Father Ranganathan yet about the funeral?"

"No, I will speak to Tony about the arrangements."

"Let me know if I can be of any help, Arvind. Tony has done a lot for Marsti and everyone is with him in this time."

"I still can't believe something like this could have happened to our Sam. We just celebrated her birthday last month, Doc!"

"Hmmm... I will see you," said Dr Sumanth, lost for words to express his own feelings of dismay and shock, sweating at the thought of explaining to Tony what had actually happened with this little child.

He looked again at the copy of post mortem reports, x-rays, and MRI's in his hand. He had hoped Dr Moore could do the explaining to this father, but she hadn't come in yet.

"Well, someone has to talk to him and tell him the truth!" Dr Sumanth said to no one in particular, cursing Dr Moore unconsciously for not being there.

14th September
Wednesday

Tony rushed out of his car towards his front door, fidgeting with the keys, trying to put the right one in the lock. He couldn't see anything through the tears in his eyes. He thought it was a miracle that he had reached home without killing everyone in his path or himself.

The keys dropped out of his hand and as he bent to retrieve them, the bile he was holding back in his throat broke the barrier and spewed out of his mouth and on his pants before he directed it away from himself.

When he couldn't puke anymore, the tears started flowing freely. He sat back with hands hugging his knees.

He tried to get up, but his knees were too weak to support him. Getting on his knees, Tony entered the correct key in the door lock, and crawled inside on his hands and knees. Shutting the door behind, so no one could hear anymore, Tony wailed his heart out! He sat there with his back to the closed door, lights still turned off in the house, for over an hour. At some point, he lay down on the floor and cried himself to sleep.

Tony woke up a couple of hours later. Getting up slowly, Tony switched on the light and walked to the bathroom where he splashed water on his face, hard. He walked to the kitchen, poured himself a glass of Teacher's whiskey, downed it in one big sip and poured another.

Picking up his laptop from the study table, Tony walked to the sofa and turned on the television. He chose the 'Backup' option and started watching the same videos he had been watching every day since his wife had passed away eight months ago.

"I lost her Angela!" he yelled to the empty room, downed the glass of whiskey again and got up to retrieve the bottle from the kitchen counter.

I will just watch the videos for a little while, he thought to himself, and tears started flowing down his face again as he heard his daughter laughing at being tickled by Angela in the video.

"Sammy...," he moaned without realizing, as he dropped on the sofa and looked at the laughing faces of his wife and daughter. His wife was wearing her pink spaghetti top, too modern to be considered appropriate for a lady constable in Marsti. It had been her impulse buy the day before, and his daughter looked like a doll dressed in a red and purple frock that brought out the colour in her cheeks, with a pair of yellow shoes that squeaked with each step. They had made Sam jump around in delight all day, making music of her own.

It had been their first vacation out of Marsti. Sam had been delighted at her experience of being at sea. They had hired a motorboat with a driver and sailed, fished, had lunches on the beach, lazed around at the hotel in afternoons, gone out eating at different restaurants in the evening. Sam had not made a fuss or cried during the whole trip.

He had recorded this particular video on their second day at Paradise beach. Angela had been the one complaining about the sun being too strong to go to the beach after 11 a.m. and Tony had agreed, but Sam was hell bent on making a sand castle with her dada and that had made his decision.

Angela was trying to keep an umbrella over Sam as she applied sunscreen on her. Tony hadn't been able to control his laugh because the umbrella kept slipping away from between her shoulder and head in the strong wind and when Angela had tried to hold the umbrella with one hand, Sam had tried to slip away from her mother. "It smells so bad, Amma!" she complained and Angela, sternly, trying to hold her own laugh in check, told her that she knew it didn't smell at all because it was non-scented.

"Will you stop recording and help me with this daughter of yours!?" Angela scolded him in the video. "Nope, you will put sunscreen on me too Ma, I am not coming close to you," Tony had teased in a childlike voice and continued to record.

When Sammy made a face at Angela, she had started to tickle her as punishment and Sammy had returned the favour, resulting in both of them rolling in the sand and the umbrella finally flying away.

Tony had recorded it all, not knowing that their paradise would soon turn to hell, and his pain just wouldn't end.

Angela had been diagnosed with last stage cancer a week later.

She was given three to six months to live, but only if she chose to get operated immediately and agreed to go through chemo and radio therapy.

She had cried, prayed, begged for Tony to save her, wondered how her daughter would grow up without a mother. She had even tried to talk Tony into marrying again to give Sam a mother, but Tony had put an end to the talk by kissing her hard.

"You are the only woman for me and I will be the mother to our child as well as a father. I promise."

The next morning, Angela had told the doctor that she wanted to spend her last days in her own house, taking care of her family. The doctor had to relent on her persistence.

Back in Marsti, her health had deteriorated quickly. Now, he sat there on the sofa, drinking, the look of defeat on his face, replaying the same video and thinking about his daughter, and his beautiful loving wife, over and over again till he dozed off. Only to be woken by his constantly recurring nightmare.

"Dada! Dada!" cried Sam as she was stuffed in a gunny sack and thrown in a haphazardly dug grave. It was dark and there was no one to hear her screams and sobs, as soil was shoved on her and as the grave was filling up, her cries became muffled moans and were snuffed out completely like her breathing must have! In this nightmare, Tony saw everything from far away and wanted to run to save his daughter, but couldn't move! He wanted to shout out to the person to let his daughter go. He wanted to kill the bastard and save his daughter, but he was immobile, without a voice.

Every time tony slept, he had the same nightmare and he woke up shouting Sam's name, every single time.

Arvind had offered to make the funeral arrangements and Tony had accepted, thankful.

The wake was the next day and funeral the day after. Arvind had also suggested that it be a closed coffin vigil at church.

Having lost all faith in the goodness of god since Angela's death, Tony had wanted nothing to do with the church, but his wife had been a devout catholic and Sam had been baptized soon after birth at Angela's insistence. If god did exist, then Sam will be next to him, and in this hope Tony had decided to follow all the catholic rites of passage.

Tony went to Sam's room to pick out her best white, Sunday frock with purple flowers. He switched on the corridor lights, but left Sam's room lights off. This was the first time he was entering Sam's room since Saturday. As he walked to the cupboard and removed her dress, he could see just enough in the gloom that filtered from the landing lights, and rushed out of the room before his eyes picked out anything else.

He dropped the dress on the dining table. Arvind would be coming in the morning and he could pick out Sam's socks and shoes. The fragrance of Sam's baby powder, her glues and paints had been overwhelming for Tony!

He picked up his laptop and started reading the evidence report again. He couldn't understand what he was missing. The panchnama was next and then he read the postmortem report again, and the pictures of Sam's broken, bloodied body made him throw the whiskey glass on the floor, again.

"Baby, I am so sorry, my baby. I am so sorry Sammy. I am so sorry Sammy. I am so so so sorry, my baby," he kept on repeating, softly at first and then louder, and louder, as if his apology would be heard above the thunder and rains outside.

15th-16th September
Thursday and Friday

Tony opened the door to let Arvind in. Arvind went in to collect Sam's shoes and socks while Tony showered and popped a Disprin to stop his headache.

People were spilling on the road when they reached, and against his wish, Tony entered and sat on the last bench. The church was full of people he knew and some that he didn't know, wearing black, teary-eyed. He didn't want to look at any of their faces and see the sorrow etched there, his own sorrow was being contained by sheer will. Tony couldn't even bear to look at the closed casket that Sammy now lay in. The rapist had disfigured her face and most of her teeth were broken.

Tony distanced himself by thinking about his daughter's first day at school. She had not cried, nor had been scared. Brave little Sammy had been waiting for school to open for a whole month, taking out her school bag and arranging and rearranging her books every day.

When Tony had dropped her at the gate, she had kissed him on his forehead, he had returned the kiss and she had run inside the school, laughing.

Sam had cried for weeks after Angela passed away. She was told her mother was with god now. Then one day she had come into Tony's room to find him crying, and asked why he was sad. "I miss your mom, Sammy," Tony had said and hugged her. They had sat like that, with the father's head on his daughter's shoulder, she comforting, and him crying. She had consoled him like a mother that day, and thereafter had taken up the role of Tony's guardian.

After that day, every morning she woke up herself, picked the newspaper from the porch, came into his room and woke him up with a kiss. She had brushed, bathed, and even had wanted to comb her own hair, but always ended up tangling her long hair in the brush instead. After Angela, Tony had learnt quickly how to comb her beautiful, soft hair and make breakfast and the other meals, which usually turned to be pancakes, Sam's favourite. She could be a bully when she wanted to be. But always well-mannered and had never done anything Tony had asked her once not to.

She had once burned her fingers trying to help Tony in the kitchen, picking up a hot pan from the kitchen platform. Tony had told her never to enter the kitchen again till she was older and Sam never did. She sat on the other side of the open kitchen counter and always asked her dada if she could help in any way, but had never even crossed to the other side.

She had never complained about anything. The only exception being her complaining that Julie scared her and had told her off for not listening to her. Tony had been able to reason with his daughter that Julie was only looking out for her interest and to not argue with her. Acting years ahead of her age, Sam had not only understood, but had also apologized to Julie.

She was a perfect angel!

Was. Breaking his own train of thoughts, tears came uninvited to his eyes.

At the altar, Father Ranganathan was reading from the holy book and everyone's eyes were moist, some held napkins to occasionally wipe their cheeks, looking back at Tony every now and then, with pathetic morose smiles. He wanted to shout at everyone and ask them where they were when his child was dying? Why hadn't anyone helped her!?

Where was I when you were being hurt, baby? Why couldn't I hear your cries? Why am I not dead instead of you? Tony couldn't take it anymore. He rushed out of the church. At the gate, he lit a cigarette and stood against the wall. He had failed as a father in his own eyes.

Feeling like a man stuck in an endless nightmare that his life had become, Tony went through the rest of the day in a daze. He drank himself unconscious upon being dropped home by Leslie.

Arvind picked him up the next day for the funeral and drove to the cemetery.

Tony hoped against hope, to wake up any moment, to realize this was all just a bad dream.

He was standing at the back of the over-crowded grave site, glassy eyed and stinking of stale whiskey, when Mrs Krishnan, clad in a white saree, eyes bright and dynamic, approached him to comfort the grieving father. The tall, big woman, walked with the grace of a tiger, and spoke with a voice that was commanding without trying.

"Are you okay, Tony?" she asked concerned. Tony looked pale-faced, ready to faint, or throw up, or both.

"Yes," he grunted.

"I know this is the worst time for you, Tony, but you have to stay strong."

Tony just made a sound in his throat in acknowledgment of having heard her, without looking at her. He continued to look into the space above her shoulder.

"Tony, you should say a few words for Samantha," she said putting a hand on his shoulder.

At the mention of Sam, Tony looked at Mrs Krishnan as if she had jerked him awake.

"I understand your pain, but you owe her that, Tony."

When Tony just stared at her, she continued in a softer, more comforting tone, "I have a daughter too, Tony, and..." she stopped at the look that had crept into Tony's eyes. He looked murderous.

His forehead creased, tears now starting to flow from his eyes, a tick had started in his jaw as he clenched it, "Mind your own fucking business and leave me alone!" Tony said loud enough for everyone gathered to hear.

Shocked, Mrs Krishnan started to say something again when Tony cut her off, "Your daughter is safe at home while mine lies in that coffin. Do you know why it was a closed casket service? Because the doctor couldn't sew her up well enough where she had been cut with blades, because the mortician didn't think he could put anything that would hide all the marks on her body. My daughter was only six years old, and she was hurt in places she didn't even know existed. Don't bloody tell me you understand shit! Just *leave me the fuck alone!"* and stalked off without a backward glance.

17th September
Saturday

As Tony entered the police station the next morning, it was evident to Arvind that he had had a rough night.

"Are you okay, Tony?" Arvind asked softly.

"Hmm," said Tony without looking at him and walked to his cabin.

After what Dr Sumanth had told them on Wednesday, Arvind had had nightmares worse than any he had as a child.

Sam had been mutilated, beaten and scratched! And there was something even worse: she had been raped and in the most brutal manner.

He had read about many rape cases and each one was brutal. But never had Arvind imagined something like this happening to someone so close to him, and in Marsti. The only major crime that was committed here was years ago, when a woman had killed her lover by stabbing him. Since then, the only crimes were theft or drunk driving and mostly those involved were not locals.

He kept thinking about what the postmortem report had showed; what Dr Sumanth had said. The doctor himself had been unable to hold his tears back, for the fate of the innocent child, or the hatred for the killer, out of his voice.

Dr Sumanth had said that her body had gone into severe dehydration on the second day after being kidnapped, probably from crying, and possibly because she was given little or no water to drink, but the child had been strong and the dehydration hadn't been able to kill her.

The child had been put through hell; she had been raped after torturing the child for more than two days, when the monster was done with her, he had stuffed her in a gunny sack and had thrown her in the woods. Maybe the killer had thought her to be dead in that comatose state, but she still had life left in her. It was a wonder that the animals hadn't got to her while she lay there, breathing her last breaths. Between being dumped there and next morning, when the vacationing college kids had found her, she had breathed her last.

The postmortem revealed that her lungs were full of dust and she died of excessive bleeding.

"I will kill you, you monster! I will find you and kill you!" Arvind muttered under his breath, loud enough for Leslie to hear, who looked at him in shock and fear, as if he had lost his mind.

Doctor had told them that traces of a sedative were found in Sam's blood. Her internal organs were damaged due to forceful entry and the blood loss had been severe. Dr Sumanth was surprised that there were no semen traces at all; he assumed that the killer had most probably worn gloves to avoid finger prints. The bite marks on the body would also need to be tested against a suspect to be sure that he was the culprit. He had collected DNA from the bite marks. Only problem was that there was no suspect yet!

Dr Sumanth had said that she probably wasn't raped where her body was found, it had to have been a dry and dusty place. Her clothes were not soiled but dusty.

There was no soil on her body from the woods, but he couldn't be sure unless he consulted a forensics expert. The body, he surmised, must have been dumped after 3.00 a.m. on Tuesday, 13th September, based on the fact that it had rained till midnight heavily and drizzled till about 1 a.m. and Sam wasn't left on a very wet ground, but just damp, or she would have been soaked, but wasn't. The time of death was anywhere between 7.00 am to 10.00 a.m. based on the fact that the body was in the stage of autolysis when bought in for postmortem, at 2.00 p.m.

"Oh, my darling, poor child..." Arvind started to clench his fist again, the phone on Leslie's desk rang and surprised, she knocked her penholder as she jumped. Collecting himself, Arvind unclenched his fist and let out the breath he was holding and walked into Tony's cabin.

"Sir, Dr Sumanth called; he has sent samples of Sam's blood, the dust found in the nostrils and lungs, the gunny bag, as well as the soil from woods to the toxicologist and forensic expert he knows in Delhi. He said this doctor is his friend, he will start the tests as soon as he receives the samples tomorrow and send the report without delay."

"Okay. Arvind, I have gone over all the evidence and reports, over and over again, and I can't make anything out of it. I want you to walk through it with me. Maybe we will find something together that I haven't been able to see by myself."

"Okay sir, I have read the reports too and one thing is for sure, I also think that Sam wasn't raped where we found her.

I don't know about the dust and all, but we had gone through every inch of the jungle as if with a comb. Sam was definitely not in the woods on Saturday or Sunday. We were searching hotels in and around Marsti on Monday, so that must be when she was left there."

"Victim," said Tony in a voice so low that Arvind looked up questioningly.

"Victim," Tony shouted, "Don't say her name."

Embarrassed, Arvind looked away from Tony's eyes and muttered, "Yes sir."

"Bring me the town map," said Tony.

Arvind promptly spread it out on the table.

"Okay, so we found the body here, it's about 5 kms from my house, 7 kms from Mr Ananth's and 10 kms from David's. There is a river here at another 7.5 kms that goes right through to the west and ends at sunset cliff into a waterfall," Tony said marking each with an 'X'. "There are only six houses on this street – Amanda's, David's guesthouse, David's bungalow, mine, Mr Ananth's and 15 kms away on the east is where Leslie stays now. Did you check the guesthouse?"

"No sir."

"We will check it today, and..." there was a knock on the door

Leslie came in, "Sir, I was going to get myself some coffee, would you like some?" she asked reticently.

"No Leslie, but come in for a minute please. You were on David's search team. Did your group search his guesthouse on Saturday or Sunday?"

"No, sir. I didn't think it needed to be searched. I was told nobody went there. I thought it is haunted; we searched all around it, but I don't think anyone went to look inside. Shall I call everyone and check if anyone searched inside, sir? I am so sorry sir... I didn't know I was to check it, nobody told me sir..."

Tony interrupted her rant. "Leslie! I just asked if it was searched. Come here and have a look at this map. Are you sure other than the guesthouse, you didn't miss any other place? Where is your map? Get it!"

Leslie rushed to get the map she had been given during the search that had started on Saturday night and lasted till Sunday evening, by when more than half the town had joined in at Mayor Krishnan's behest.

"Arvind, we will go and check out the spot where we found the victim, and David's guesthouse."

"Now sir?"

"No, tomorrow. Does that work for you?"

"Sorry, sir." Leslie came in carrying the map, and trying to spread it on the table, she knocked over the pen stand, the paper weight, and was about to knock the table lamp off when Arvind pushed it out of harm's way.

"Leslie, you can leave. We will manage. Thank you," Tony said exasperated.

"Sorry sir, I will pick up this..," Leslie bent to pick up the pen stand, pens and paper weight and while getting up, banged her head on the table.

"Ow!" she yelped.

"Sorry sir," said Leslie once again and left the room looking dejected.

They had been talking for only about ten minutes when the constable came in to inform them about a theft case.

Tony asked Arvind to enquire what the matter was.

It was past 5.00 p.m. when they left for the woods. After searching the surrounding areas of the crime scene, and finding nothing, they headed for David's guesthouse.

Arvind searched the first floor and Tony inspected the ground and basement. The sun was low enough that they had to use torches to see well.

Arvind came down after sometime and told Tony that there was nothing suspicious there, but the first floor looked like it had been cleaned recently. "You can still smell the cleansing agent. No cigarette butts or empty beer bottles or chip bags. Nothing. It's all been cleared out."

"That's odd. Why would he have the first floor cleaned and not the ground? And why have this place cleaned at all? Is he planning on starting this place again?"

"I don't think so, sir. The town council will never permit it. And Mrs Krishnan has made it clear at several council meetings that she thinks even his bar should be shut down."

"I will need to speak to David." Tony said as he climbed the stairs to check the upper floor himself. He walked into the first room, which still had the marks from where the bed must have stood. A broken cupboard stood in a corner with doors standing ajar and shelves fallen down inside. He scanned the room carefully. Something was not right here, but he couldn't understand what. He stood in the center of the room, looking at the ceiling towards the fan motor with missing blades, for all of two minutes, and suddenly he realized it – the floors were clean, as if scrubbed, but the ceilings, the fan, the broken tubelights and the windows were as dirty as ever.

Removing his phone from his back pocket, he called David, his face set hard as stone.

"What happened, sir?" Arvind asked, but got no reply.

"Hello? Is this David's phone?" he asked curtly. After a brief pause, he continued, "I need to speak to him as soon as he wakes up. Tell him Inspector Anthony George called and ask him to come by the police station by himself or I will have to come and get him."

A tick had started in his jaw again; Arvind followed him wordlessly, as he searched every room, more thoroughly than Arvind had.

The sun had set, the twilight had come and turned to night. When they both walked out of the guesthouse and towards the police jeep, the moon had risen.

"Sir, you don't think David had anything to do with this, do you? He might be a drunk, but he hasn't even been accused of misbehaving with a woman, ever," Arvind asked finally when they were driving back.

"I don't know what I am thinking, Arvind. Call Dr Sumanth, have him collect the samples and send them to that forensics expert."

"Where was David, Tony sir, when you called?"

"He is at home. His maid answered the call. He was drinking all day and is passed out drunk, as always."

"Shall we pick him up, sir?"

"No. He will be able to answer nothing right now. He is hardly coherent when in his senses, and I need some straight answers when he is awake and has his bearings."

Arvind called Dr Sumanth to ask him when he could collect samples from David's guesthouse and was told that the toxicologist's reports had been sent to them by email. The report confirmed his suspicions that the traces of dust found in Sam's body were not the same as the soil from the woods.

He told Arvind that he could reach in an hour to collect the samples from David's guesthouse that very night. Arvind dropped Tony home and took the jeep back to the guesthouse to meet Dr Sumanth.

18th September
Sunday

Sunil came in as soon as the sun was up. Riding his second-hand scooty, he had covered the 25 kms from his home to the police station in just over half an hour.

His friends had warned him against it, but he couldn't stay quiet anymore. He had to tell Tony sir what he had seen. What his friends and he had witnessed. He was scared, but determined.

What Tony sir had done for him had changed his life, not completely, but for the best. He had saved Sunil from years in jail for theft and drugs, his mother from loneliness and misery, and that day Sunil had decided to turn his life around. He was studying better now. Since then, Sunil had taken up a job in David's bar, and was trying to quit drugs too.

Almost a year had passed since he had last entered this police station, in cuffs, but this time Sunil had walked in out of his own accord. He was waiting since 7.00 am, anxiously. Many a time he had thought of just walking out, but he couldn't turn his back on Tony sir's kindness by hiding something that might be important in solving Sam's murder. This was the least he could do.

Tony came around 10.30 and headed for his cabin without looking at Sunil.

Tony was looking at the picture of his wife and daughter when there was a knock on the door. He put the picture back in his desk drawer and yelled, "What?!"

Arvind slowly opened the door and ducked his head in, "May I come in, sir?"

"Yes!" came the curt reply

"Are you okay, Tony sir?"

He looked up, sighed and replied in a calmer tone now, "Yes Arvind, I am fine. Stop asking me the same damn question ten times every day! What do you want?"

"Sir, Sunil Anand is here. He wants to talk to you; says it's urgent."

"Call him in."

Arvind opened the door of Tony's cabin and called out Sunil's name.

Sunil got up and walked towards Tony's cabin. The woman on the desk across from him, in constable's uniform of khaki dress, had seemed familiar to Sunil, but he couldn't place her. With dry messy hair tied in a bun, heavy kajal in her eyes that was already smeared, no jewellry or make up, save for the big 'bindi' on her forehead, she looked like any other woman, but there was just something about her. What, he didn't know. When Sunil had tried to make eye contact and smile, she had nervously looked down. The phone had rung at the same time and she had jumped like someone had burst firecrackers under her chair.

Sunil dragged his eyes away from her and with heavy feet walked into Tony's cabin, looking down and telling himself under his breath, "It has to be done! There's no other choice. This is the right thing to do!"

"Sit!" said Tony when he saw Sunil.

"Sir, good morning sir," he said and then cursed himself. It wasn't a good morning for Tony sir!

"I have something to confess and something to tell you, but please sir," he spoke hurriedly before Tony could say anything, "I have not robbed anyone after that day, sir. I swear. I have taken a job at the David sir's bar and that's how I could afford it and I am trying to quit anyway. Please don't tell David sir, or I will lose my job, sir! My friends told me that I should just keep my mouth shut, but I couldn't, after what you have done for me sir. I didn't know sir, or I would have done something. I swear sir! I had no idea, sir. None of us did. But I am sorry sir. I am really very sorry, sir. But I just didn't know sir!" he blabbered fast and immediately looked down at his own feet, breathing hard, as if he had run a marathon.

"What are you talking about, Sunil!?"

"Sir, before I say anything, I have to request that me, or my friends will not be punished for doing drugs."

"If you don't speak clearly, I promise, you will be worse than punished, Sunil!"

Looking as if he had made a mistake by coming at all, Sunil looked from Tony to Arvind and back; there was no way out now.

Sunil took a deep breath and started narrating, "Sir, me and my friends saw someone in the woods on Monday early morning and Tuesday too."

Sunil told Tony exactly what they saw in the woods early Monday morning and that day after college.

"Winston's father had been summoned by the principal, and he took him home directly. We couldn't reach him on his cell phone till nine in the evening. After his father had beaten him and mother done crying, he was excused to his room. From there he had called me and Chris to say he wouldn't be able to come out till his parents got over their anger."

Sunil and Chris left for David's guesthouse to retrieve their stash of weed around 1 a.m. and had reached on foot by 2.30 a.m.

"We didn't want to dilly dally around after our last experience. We were still spooked, so me and Chris went straight in to retrieve the stash and get out of there.

"We heard some shuffling as soon as we entered. We both halted, sir. We could hear footsteps on the the first floor. Sir, no one goes to the first floor; it's empty, sir. There is no furniture upstairs either, apart from a few broken chairs and an old cupboard with broken doors."

Tony got up from his seat, opened his desk drawer and took out his gun. Sunil blanched, and trying to scramble off the chair, he almost fell out of his seat thinking Tony was going to shoot him, but Tony holstered his gun and Sunil let out a loud sigh of relief. He had been listening to Sunil's account with confusion at first and then his features had started to contort into something that neither Sunil nor Arvind could place exactly. On his face was the look of anger, horror, regret, and something else that was more difficult to place, something more sinister.

"Arvind, I am going to the guesthouse. Sunil, call Chris and Winston and ask them to come to the guesthouse too," Tony said, his voice calm.

"Sir, please, we don't want to be in any trouble, and if David sir found out that we hid weed in his guesthouse, he will throw me out. We didn't see anything else, sir, please don't involve us, sir. I just wanted to help, sir. If my mom finds out I was doing drugs again, she will be very disappointed. Please, Tony sir. I swear we don't know anything else, sir!"

"Shut up and call them. Come on! We are going now."

Obediently, Sunil stopped blabbering, scared. He followed Tony, and called Chris and Winston from the mobile phone Tony handed him.

18th September
Sunday

The road leading to David's guesthouse passed from his palatial bungalow that was in a worse for wear state now and needed almost as much repair as the old guesthouse did. The colour had faded from white to a dirty off white, the plaster breaking down in places, patchwork due to leakages were clearly seen in places, some steps were broken and even the driveway leading to the house had potholes in it.

Tony halted at David's house to pick him up, but was told by the maid that he was at the bar. Tony called David and told him to come to the guesthouse immediately.

A ten-minute drive took them outside the guesthouse. It looked really haunted to Sunil now, even in broad daylight, given the recent events he had witnessed there. The large house that had once been the pride of late Arthur D'mello, David's father, lay in shambles. Broken windowpanes, colourless walls except for the brick and wood shade of earthy brown, that too was covered in moss after the heavy rains of the past few months. There was weed growing out of the house itself as well. It was unbelievable that this place had once been a host to some of south India's biggest businessmen and dignitaries.

"Now walk me through exactly what happened the next night, step by step. Tell me precisely what you spoke and what you did and where you stood and what you heard," Tony said, all business.

"Okay sir, so we came walking from mall road from that direction," Sunil said pointing towards the east. "I got off work around 12.30, but it was drizzling and quite cold, so we decided to have a few beers before we started. It took us over an hour and a half, so we must've reached around 3.00, I think..."

"How much did you drink that night?"

"I don't remember for sure, sir. David sir allows all the employees to have two beers after work for free every week," said Sunil looking at his feet. He respected Tony sir and was thankful and all, but this huge man scared him too.

"Think and tell me Sunil!"

"Four, maybe five... Eight maybe... among both of us... I can check at the bar, employee or not, free beer or not, we are supposed to log in everything. The manager at David sir's bar is very particular about it."

"Okay, continue."

"Sir, we entered and were walking towards that cabinet," said Sunil, standing just inside the door and pointing towards a heavy cabinet that was overturned on its side, "when we both heard footsteps coming from above," he said looking now towards the staircase leading from the entryway upstairs. "We stood still, listening for about thirty seconds or a minute and then ran out." Sunil walked back out and pointed towards a huge tree surrounded by tall grass and wild bushes. "We hid behind there."

He shifted from one foot to another. "We should have gone home or checked who was upstairs, but we were really scared sir. I am scared of ghosts and I think Chris is too."

"What happened then?"

"We sat here for about half an hour. I know it was 3.35 a.m. because I checked my watch. But we didn't see or hear anything. Thinking that it may have been a mouse or something, we decided to just get our stuff and get out of here.

"As we were about to get up, we saw someone come out the door. It was cloudy and dark, sir, so we couldn't see the face."

"What did you see? How do you know it was the same person you had seen the night before?"

"Sir, he was wearing the same clothes, a black hoodie pulled down covering his face. He was fat and short and I saw his military shoes. This time I made sure I saw the feet to confirm that it was human," Sunil said embarrassed, but continued. "He was wearing military shoes, sir, the ones with heavy soles!" Sunil looked up as if this was a big clue.

"Continue, Sunil."

"Sir, then the man walked in that direction," he pointed towards the north. "We thought it was probably a thief or a new watchman or something, because we knew it wasn't a ghost and we were relieved, but we didn't want to be seen yet, so we waited for him to leave and after another ten minutes when no one else came out, we went inside, got our weed and ran home."

He paused for a bit. "Sir, this guy we saw was carrying a gunny sack on his shoulder," he said almost guiltily.

Tony looked like someone had drained all the colour out of his face. "Are you sure, Sunil? Are you absolutely sure?"

"Yes sir, and I am sorry sir, I didn't know Samantha had gone missing or I would have reported what I saw immediately. I am very sorry sir. I really didn't know," Sunil muttered close to tears now. "I would have informed you and she would be alive. I would have done something, sir. I just didn't know. I really had no idea, none of us did. We would have done something sir. I am so sorry Tony sir," Sunil finished, crying freely now.

Tony took out his phone and dialled a number, "Where have you reached, David?" he asked in a calm tone but his eyes were murderous.

Sunil had recently found out that Sam had been dumped in a gunny bag and knew that the man they had seen was probably the killer. Sunil had also heard that his daughter had been alive when she was dumped in the woods. Sunil felt guilty that he hadn't done something to stop the man.

When Winston had told him what he had heard from his father who worked in the town council, they had put two and two together. They had talked about how they should've done something on Sunday or at least followed the man on Tuesday morning and checked what was in the sack he was carrying.

Tony shoved the phone in Sunil's face, breaking his remorseful thoughts and asked him to call Chris and Winston. He did as was told. His friends would reach in ten more minutes. They were coming on Winston's scooty, he told Tony.

Sunil was still sobbing when Tony said, "It's done now Sunil; don't beat yourself about what can't be changed. Thank you for coming and telling me what you saw."

"I am sorry, sir."

"How far is the place where you saw this man running on Monday?" Tony asked to change the subject, not wanting to blame this kid whose only fault was witnessing something he hadn't understood, but feeling angry, nonetheless.

"Ten... maybe fifteen minutes' walk, sir."

An old Mercedes C class pulled over next to Tony's jeep and an already inebriated David got out, dropped his car keys, picked them up and walked towards Tony, enquiringly and looking pissed.

David had just won three back to back games when he had received a call from Tony, who had ordered David here. He would've told Tony to fuck off, but he didn't want to get on the wrong side of the townspeople anymore. They were just looking for an excuse to shut down his bar. David walked towards Tony, who was looking as if he owned the land he stood on, with hands folded across his chest.

"What are you doing here, Tony?" asked David folding his own hands across his own chest. His beer belly stretching his shirt buttons dangerously, he stood a foot shorter than Tony.

"I am waiting for a tour of your guesthouse, David," Tony said flatly.

"What? Why?"

"Let's walk inside, David. I am going to tell you everything and so are you, now!"

David looked unbelievingly at Tony but walked inside the guesthouse.

"So what do you want to see, Officer George?" asked David mockingly, raising both his hands and waving them around in welcome.

"Where did you keep your 'stuff' Sunil?" Tony asked and David looked at Sunil, just realizing he was present too.

Looking like a deer caught in headlights, Sunil pointed toward the overturned cabinet again. Tony walked towards it and examined the small area where the dust was disturbed due to the constant displacement of the cabinet. It was too minute to be noticed otherwise. "What stuff?" demanded David of Sunil now who cast his eyes low.

David hadn't noticed it then, Tony guessed. If he had known someone was coming here regularly, he would have chosen another place, or locked the house against intruders.

"David, why don't you keep this dump locked?"

"I had tried a few times, but the kids broke the lock each time and what is there to lock anyway? Most of the furniture has been carried away by thieves, or broken, and thanks to the town council, I can't run a business here."

Tony nodded but David wasn't behaving like a guilty man would, and this was putting doubts in Tony's mind. He had been sure that David was the killer after hearing Sunil's account. He had even decided how he was going to beat David within an inch of his life, and nurse him back, and beat him again and repeat till he begged to be killed, but David looked more irritated than scared, or even worried.

Tony quickly walked into the room that used to be the kitchen and then ran down the basement, as he had the evening before. He knew this guesthouse from having raided it for illegal activities involving drugs and prostitution before it was shut down. There was nothing out of place here other than the place being a run-down wreck.

"Let's walk upstairs now, shall we David?"

"What is this about, Tony? What have I done now? And what is this bartender doing here?"

"Just keep shut and walk," Tony directed.

Sunil in the lead, followed by David and Tony, the three climbed the stairs and were hit by, strong smell of house cleaners immediately.

"Have you had the house cleaned, David?" Tony asked, observing David keenly.

"No! Some kids must've spilled something..." but even David knew the strong smell of phenol and cleaning bleaches that lingered in the musty air.

Tony noticed that the stairs landing had stains on either sides but were clean from between, "Did you have the rug here removed?" Tony asked.

"No! Someone must have stolen it," replied David, scared now. He had noticed that too, and also that the dusty railings were not dusty anymore. In fact, as they reached the first floor, he realized that the stairs and the first floor, where the guestrooms used to be, were as clean as ever.

"Why are we here, Tony?"

"We will know in a bit, David. Show us every room."

There were six rooms on the first floor of David's guesthouse. His father had meant it to be just that, a place for guests to stay at when they had their lavish parties. This was before his father had been taken ill and passed away, leaving everything to David.

Led by David now, the trio scanned every room, each as keenly as the other. Every room was empty, spare a chair here, a broken cupboard, or a rusted bed there, or the smelly, stained bedding that had been used by teens even after the place had been shut for years. There were two bathrooms, each on the ground floor and first, and as they approached the one at the far end of the corridor, the smells of cleaning liquids hit them, strong enough for each to scrunch their noses. The spacious bathroom had a small cabinet below the washbasin, and a pot next to it, a bathtub, and a shower cubicle. The bathroom on the ground floor had been dirty, but the one on this floor had been scrubbed clean, and was sparkling now.

"David?" asked Tony.

"I don't know Tony! I didn't have anybody clean up. You know nobody is ready to work here anymore, not after the last watchman died. There were all these rumors and nobody wanted to come here to work even for more money. Must be some kids. I can't think of anything else."

"David, you're coming with me to the police station."

"What for? I haven't done anything Tony! And it's not a crime to have a clean place." David's face was ashy, a look of despair and disbelief on his face, his bloodshot eyes alert. "I don't understand what is happening. What have I done?!"

Tony suddenly pounced on him. From being quiet and cool, he was suddenly ferocious, "David, you will come with me to the station without any fuss, and you will answer all my questions, not ask them, or you will regret ever being born," he said and the tone sent prickles up and down Sunil and David's spines.

"This is wrong! You are misusing your uniform. I haven't done anything," said David, frantically.

As they came out, they saw Winston's scooty parked next to the porch and Winston and Chris huddled together.

"David, wait in my jeep now. Okay?" Tony said while handcuffing David. Tony then pulled David by the cuffs, locked the other end of handcuffs on the jeep door, leaving a bewildered David without a backward glance. He walked towards Winston and Chris, who were looking as if their death was approaching.

"Let's go to where you saw that man running that day and I want you all to tell me exactly what you saw, said and did." He motioned for them to lead and they did quietly, doubtfully and accusingly looking at Sunil, but careful not to catch Tony's eye.

19th September Monday

"Sir, do you really think David has done this?" Arvind asked Tony when he came out of the police station room where David was kept. Tony hadn't gone home all night. He had already questioned David thrice, alone, since he was brought in. The night constable was instructed to not let David sleep and he hadn't been given any food or water.

"It's 6 a.m. Call his girlfriend Catherine Xavier and Dr Moore. Don't tell either that David has been arrested, but tell them to come by 8 a.m."

"Okay sir."

"And send in some water and food for David. Let him sleep if he wishes to."

"Okay sir." Arvind nodded.

"Tony sir, you should sleep for some time too," Arvind said timidly, concerned for Tony; he looked like a mad man under attack.

Without saying another word, Tony walked into his cabin. He poured himself a drink, lit a cigarette, and took a deep drag.

Dr Moore came before 8.00 a.m. and Arvind regretfully woke up Tony.

"Tony, is everything okay? Is this about Sammy? Did you find something, dear?"

Tony pulled up the chair for Dr Moore as she walked into his cabin, and poured a glass of water for her. In her early fifties, Dr Collette Moore looked more like sixty, and spoke to everyone, patients and friends, like a mother would to a child. The pale salwar kameez was pressed well, but hung lose from her shoulders. Her hair was wisp thin, and the flyaway had already escaped her tight bun, and were curling around her forehead. She took a seat and smiled her kind smile looking up at Tony and said, "You need to rest, my dear. Looks like you haven't slept in days. You have a lot to do, and falling sick will only slow you down."

Taking a seat from across her, Tony simple asked, "When did you last see David, Collette?"

The expression on her serene face changed to that of anxiety, "Is he okay, Tony? Is something wrong with David?" she enquired, on the edge of her chair.

"David is fine, Collette. When did you see him last?"

"Sunday, not yesterday, last Sunday. Why are you asking, Tony? What has happened? Has he done something again?"

"Why did you meet him on Sunday? Where? And till what time were you with him?"

"Tony, you are scaring me!"

"Please just answer me, Collette," Tony said walking to the other side of the table and taking the seat next to Dr Moore.

"I saw David on Sunday night at his house. He was not well. His housekeeper called me around 8.00 p.m. and I stayed with him that night and the following days, that is on Monday and Tuesday. I went to the hospital in the morning and went to see him straight from there in the evenings."

"Was there anyone else with him? Or anyone who came to see him, or any unusual calls he may have received?"

"He received a couple of calls from his bar, I assume from his manager. No other calls that I remember. His girlfriend Catherine was with him all this while. In fact, they were together when I reached his house on Sunday night. Is David in some kind of trouble?" she asked, fear clearly etched in her soft features.

There was a knock, and Arvind ducked his head inside the door to say that Catherine had come.

"Ask her to wait for a bit, Arvind."

"What was David's aliment that you had to stay with him for three days, Collette?"

"I will tell you, but you have to promise you will not arrest him for it. Please, Tony," Dr Moore pleaded, and Tony nodded his yes, without a doubt now of what it could have been.

"He and Catherine had overdosed on cocaine and some other drugs," she said, looking ashamed.

"Okay. Please wait outside. Tell Arvind to get you a cup of coffee or tea, and some breakfast."

"Tony, can I meet David?"

"You can take him home in a little while, if Catherine corroborates your story."

"Tony, you know I wouldn't lie."

"I know. And I trust you. Will you trust me, please? Even if David is not connected to this, it is possible that a crime has taken place in his guesthouse, and I have to follow procedure," Tony replied calmly. "Please wait outside now, Collette."

Arvind sent in Catherine, whose character and manners were opposite of Dr Moore's. "Why have you called me here, Mr George?" she asked shortly, and walking in, took a seat without waiting for a reply. She had heavy make up on her face, eyes were puffy and wrinkled from too much alcohol, and age was catching up sooner that it should have. Bright orange lipstick was smeared on her lips and liberally applied blush on her cheeks was failing to hide her gray complexion, wearing jeans that hugged her lower body and a top that showed off more than necessary stomach flab.

"Miss Xavier, when was the last time you met David D'mello?"

Tony came out half an hour later, and told Arvind to make the report of the findings of the previous night on the basis of Sunil and his friends' account, and sent a constable to seal off the guesthouse.

David and the women were allowed to leave once the formalities were complete, but David was fuming and frothing at the mouth by then in anger. "You will pay for this Tony! You think you are strong because you have power? I will make you pay for what you have done." He was yelling as Dr Moore led him out of the police station by hand, quietly apologizing to Tony, while Catherine gave him the death stare.

"Arvind, call and record the statements of Julie, and my neighbours Mr and Mrs Ananth, and Amanda D'silva," Tony said, dismissing David's threat.

"Okay Tony," Arvind said. Tony was almost at his cabin, when turned around and told Arvind to take a couple of hours off. “Call them and ask them to come in later in the day. Go home and sleep for a few hours. You look tired.”

“You are as tired as me Tony,” Arvind started but was interrupted midsentence.

“Just go home, Arvind. I am not sleepy anyway. And this can wait for a few hours.”

“Okay. I will call them and fix the time, and head home.”

A few minutes later, Arvind came back to tell Tony that Julie would be coming in the next day as she was unwell, and Amanda was out of town and would come in for the statement once she was back. “Tony, Amanda doesn’t even know Sam is no more. She left for Pondicherry on Saturday evening to attend some event.”

“Oh,” said Tony, in the same impersonal tone. “Still record her statement. Let’s follow the procedure.”

“Okay. And Mr and Mrs Ananth will come in at 5.00 p.m. Tony, you should get some rest too. Just catch some shut eye in the storage room. There is new bedding and blankets in there. Please.”

“Arvind, leave me alone now, please,” Tony said and he obliged, disappointed.

Tony was staring out the window into space, hands clenched tight, jaw ticking again.

It had been over a week and the killer was out there somewhere, while his daughter was buried under a ton of soil. He couldn’t have slept if he wished. The nightmare that his life had become would keep him awake for a long time for the fear for letting the killer escape while he slept.

19th September
Monday night

Tony reached home after 8.00 p.m. He changed into pyjamas, and shirtless walked to the kitchen, poured some whiskey in a glass and downed it in one go. He was tired to the bone, but the emptiness of the house was haunting, and he knew sleep wouldn't come easy. He thought about watching Sam and Angela's videos again, but the memories – unforgettable and painful – made him decide otherwise. Unable to sit in the house, he carried his glass and the Teacher's whiskey bottle to the back porch.

Wanting to escape all the thoughts on his mind, he sat quietly, hearing the wind whistle in the woods and the crickets. The mosquitoes started to buzz around him soon. He got up from the steps, his eyes well-adjusted to the dark by now, walked towards the electric board. He reached behind the chairs and table arrangement that Angela had chosen herself at the cane furniture shop, and switched on the light and the electric mosquito repellant switches. On the table lay a plate with moldy sandwiches, a few bites missing from one, and Sam's water bottle with the Pokémon cartoon.

Julie had told him that she had been fixing sandwiches while Sam had played in the garden. Had Julie carried it here for Sam to find her missing? But if this plate was for Sam, then who had eaten it? Julie? Then where was Sam's plate? There had been no other plate in the kitchen or the sink that day. He would ask Julie the next day, Tony thought and went back to sit on the steps.

In the light, Tony could see that his usually well-kept garden lawn was starting to look like the woods beyond. There were patches of weed growing in the grass that he had trimmed just a few weeks back to make snakes and rats visible if they decided to visit. The rose bushes were looking wild and unkempt too. He was deciding if he should start his lawn mower to trim the grass. That way, he thought, he could tire himself out to sleep and start with pruning the plants the next day. He was looking at the frangipani tree that was planted when Angela and he had got married, as a remembrance, when he saw a pile of wilted flowers near the protruding roots; a tear escaped, followed by a sigh.

Sam must have been picking them for him, as she usually did.

But why had she dropped them like that? Sam loved flowers and to carelessly drop them on the ground after picking them up wasn't like her. Why hadn't she taken them inside the house?

Had something made her drop the flowers? Or someone?

Had someone called her or had she seen someone and gone to them?

Sam knew better than to talk to strangers. Had it been someone she knew? Tony walked to the frangipani tree hurriedly.

"Why didn't I think of it before?" he asked himself. Sam, he knew, would never talk to or go with any stranger. And she had been told clearly not to go out without her Dada or Julie. Never had Sam disobeyed Tony before. Why would she that day either? Unless she had thought it was someone she could trust!

He started to wonder if she was kidnapped from the house itself. He hadn't thought of this before.

He went inside the house and called Julie's home. It was 10.15 p.m. and her mother, Mrs Lobo picked up after several rings to say Julie was sleeping, "Should I wake her up, Tony?" she asked empathetically.

Tony realized that it would be better to ask Julie the details the next day, and if she had missed telling him something. "No, Mrs Lobo. I will speak to her tomorrow," Tony said and hung up.

He went back to the porch and sat there till the half full bottle of Teacher's was finally empty. He took the plate and Sam's water bottle into the house and left it on the kitchen counter.

Unable to bear the desolation of the house and his own state, Tony went into Sam's room and in a drunk state lay on her bed. The fragrance of her baby powder and soap still lingered in the room. He wondered how long it would be before that smell faded away into nothing, like Sammy had; he slept crying out her name again.

In early morning hours, Tony woke up to go to the washroom, in the still sleepy and very hung-over state. He came back to lie down on the bed again, holding his spinning head. His hand reached out to grab Sam's life-sized teddy, when he felt a part of the bed to be unnaturally stiff. His hand reached for the light switch, though the sun was high enough for him to be able to see and recognize what it was – dried semen.

Unable to comprehend what his eyes were seeing, unbelieving of what his mind was shouting, Tony just stood there staring at the faint stain that was burning into his retina. He rushed to the bathroom as the gravity of what he was seeing hit him. He splashed water on his face, as if to wake himself up, went back and looked at his daughter's bed again.

How was this possible! How could it be! Disoriented, disbelieving, he stood there for a long time.

Had someone come into his daughter's bedroom? But how was that possible? What had happened? Did something wrong happen to her under their own roof? Tony decided that minute that whoever had dared enter his daughter's room, was going to die.

Snapping out of the shock, and grabbing the digicam from one of the drawers in the living room, he ran back upstairs.

Tony scanned the rest of the room carefully, slowly taking every detail in, and started taking pictures of the room from every angle.

Tony searched the room, top to bottom, but found nothing else.

Pulling the bed cover, he stuffed it into a plastic bag from Sam's cupboard and carried the pillows and her soft toys to the living room.

He called Arvind to pick up Julie and her mother, and bring them to the police station immediately. He next called Dr Sumanth and asked him to reach the police station. Without brushing or taking a shower, he threw on a T-shirt lying on the table without caring if it was clean or worn. Tony carried the plastic bag and Sam's pillows to his jeep, along with her soft toys, the camera in one pocket. He drove to the police station like the devil was on his tail.

20th September
Tuesday

A crying Julie sat in the room that had become, in the last week or so, the official interrogation room. Her mother was crying too, sitting on a chair near the room door. Looking at her folded hands, eyes downcast, she kept stealing looks at Tony, who in spite of her daughter's part in the incident, had not raised his voice at Julie even once.

When Julie and her mother had come in, Tony had already been waiting and the atmosphere had been charged with anger.

"Come this way, Julie. Mrs Lobo, you can come too," he had said as he led them to the corner room down the corridor.

Julie had been quite fidgety since receiving the call the day before to come in for a statement.

This morning she had looked better, but the minute they had entered the police station, even Mrs Lobo had known that this was more than just recording Julie's statement. The stormy expression on Tony's face betrayed his calm voice. Mrs Lobo had decided immediately that she wouldn't let Tony bully her daughter. Julie was a child herself, and had gone through enough since Sam's disappearance. Julie had not eaten anything for two days after Sam was kidnapped and had stopped talking to everyone, including her friends.

When Tony's questioning started, Mrs Silvia Lobo was herself shocked with the way Julie kept dodging simple questions, and giving varying answers. A couple of times she herself had felt like asking Julie sternly to think and answer clearly, but had held herself in check.

After an hour of same questions being repeated over and over again, framed differently, and Tony calmly telling Julie over and over that she wasn't telling the whole truth, or that she was maybe forgetting something and she should think back, remember without missing any details, Julie finally broke down and started to cry.

The second shock though for Mrs Lobo was when Julie started apologizing to Tony suddenly. Tony still sat quietly, his face giving out no emotions but Mrs Lobo felt completely taken aback. "What are you apologizing for, Julie?" she asked, unable to understand, and was getting up from her chair to walk towards Julie, when Tony said 'no'. She sat down without another word.

Julie cried for another ten minutes, in which time Arvind appeared with a glasses of water for her, and her mother, and Tony.

"I am sorry Tony sir, I didn't know something like this would happen. I am really sorry, sir." Julie said in a small voice when she was finally able to speak, her voice still shaky.

"Julie, you can still right the wrong by telling me the truth, and help me catch whoever has done this. Please, don't lie anymore, child, and tell me everything. I need to find whoever has done this."

Julie finally admitted that she used to call her boyfriend Peter Sullivan over sometimes and, on this particular day, she had sent Sam to the backyard and Sam had gone missing around the afternoon.

Julie's mother was mortified after hearing the whole story. She left the police station, but not before telling Tony that he could take any legal action he saw fit for what Julie had done, and how much it had cost Tony.

"I will send Julie home with Arvind or Leslie once the formalities are completed. If she is not lying, then there is no reason to take any action against her. She may have been wrong, and might be responsible, but she is not the killer. She is also only a child. I will not take any action against her unless I have to," Tony said emotionlessly but Mrs Lobo felt the father's pain in the way the big man looked small, with his shoulders slumped, his eyes looking at his feet, his hands pulling at an imaginary hair on his palms.

"I am sorry, Tony. I am really sorry for what my daughter has done," Mrs Lobo said and rushed out of the police station.

"Arvind, pick up this Peter Sullivan and bring him in immediately. Rough him up well if he gives any trouble," Tony said in the same tone he had used with Mrs Lobo and walked to his cabin.

Arvind made a few calls and left, knowing he was going to more than rough up Peter before Tony got a chance to ask him anything.

Peter Sullivan turned out to be a hard man to find for Arvind.

Julie had told Tony that she had called Peter the night before. She had told him that her statement was going to be recorded, and that she was thinking of telling Tony the truth. Peter had tried to dissuade her and she had swayed. He had also told her he would be staying at his friend's place for a few days.

Arvind called Peter's parents, and all his friends known to his parents. He finally zeroed in on a friend who lived on mall road in the main market, close to the college, and whose parents were out of town.

At the shabby flat in one of the old buildings, Peter was holed up, high on weed. When the door was opened by Peter's friend, Arvind marched straight in to find him snorting coke off the floor. Pulling him to his feet by the collar of his open shirt, Arvind punched him in the stomach before asking, "Are you Peter?"

Dazed, hunched over, holding his stomach, Peter had nodded, feebly trying to pull free. Arvind wanted to hurt Peter more for having done something so cheap in a little girl's room, but held himself back.

Peter, dragged by his shirt, half stumbled, half crawled behind Arvind, the will to resist or even speak no longer in him. Arvind handcuffed him to the jeep seat and drove back to the police station.

"Arvind, book him for breaking and entering, and a suspect in an ongoing rape and murder investigation. Take Julie's statement too. Dr Sumanth is waiting in the interrogation room to collect his DNA samples. Put him in the lock up once he is done.

During the verbal interrogation that only needed a few slaps from Tony, Peter told him that after meeting Julie on Saturday, he had gone home straight to finish his college assignment that was due on Monday.

Tony called the Sullivans to question them next. They came in immediately, and created a scene, yelling about police brutality, the injustice, their links in high places, etc., till they were told why their son was arrested. That restrained them a little, but they still refused to believe that their only son could do something like having sex with a girl, and in a cop's house of all the places.

Tony finally called them to the newly christened interrogation room and asked them about their son's whereabouts on Saturday. They repeated Peter's story but something about their manners made Tony suspect they could be lying. Tony had to get the truth out, one way or another, and for that he needed time.

Tony held the Sullivans off till 6.00 p.m., hoping they were as moronic as their son, and past 6.00 p.m. he told them that the courts were closed for the day; they would have to pay the bail at court the next day.

This man had entered his little daughter's bedroom and dirtied it; Tony had plans for him.

Peter's parents protested when Julie was allowed to go with her mother.

After all, both were involved, they had said, and Julie had invited Peter. The girl was the culprit according to the Sullivans.

They left for home around 10.00 p.m., tired from sitting on the bench all day, hoarse from having shouted at every opportunity, thirsty and hungry. When Tony had suggested they go home and come the next day with their lawyer, they had happily obliged after seeing their son sleeping on a clean mattress with a pillow and blanket in the holding cell.

After waiting for half an hour, Tony sent the constables for a round up. Arvind made instant coffee for him and Tony, and they smoked a cigarette. They woke Peter up and took him into the interrogation room.

This time Peter told them everything, in detail.

That day, after leaving Tony's house, he and his friends had smoked up another joint in the church's old graveyard. He had told his friends in the most colourful language what his afternoon had been like. Around seven that evening, he and his two friends had driven to David's bar in his friend's car and met a girl. She was in town with her colleagues for a vacation. Peter and his friends had suggested that they take a drive and smoke a few 'doobies', and the girl had readily agreed, even though her friends had declined.

Thinking it was a good day to get lucky, they had taken her out of city limits and parked near the national highway. After a few joints shared between the girl, him, and his friends, Peter had tried to kiss the girl, but she had suddenly started shouting.

He had tried to hold her back, but without help from his friends, she had managed to get out of the car, Peter had told Tony, his cheeks red from Arvind's slaps, out of breath from a few punches he was being awarded with, every now and then.

"She started running towards the highway, trying to stop a car. So I drove back to Marsti." Another punch landed on his sides and he bawled, again.

"What was her name, and where is she now?" Tony asked without missing a beat.

"I think her name was Kavitha, and she was staying in Noble Hotel. One of my friends checked the next day, and found out that she and her friends had left."

"Now, remove your clothes and stand with your hands and legs apart," Arvind told him.

When Arvind and Tony came out, after another hour, they were sweating, and Peter was sitting in a corner of the room, naked, head bent on his knees, crying quietly.

Arvind called the wireless, after putting Peter back in the cell, and requested the constables to come back to relieve Tony and himself. "We need some rest, *thambi* or we will collapse soon," Arvind had told the head constable jokingly, when they came back. Tony had driven to his own house where Arvind stayed that night.

21st September
Wednesday

Tony and Arvind reached the police station at some time after 10.00 a.m.

Tony called Dr Sumanth to check if the toxicology reports of the samples collected from David's guesthouse had come back. "I will check Tony, and once the court grants permission, I will send Peter's samples too. I will be coming in an hour. Arvind and I are going to the court together for Peter's bail hearing. Do you plan to object his bail?"

"No doctor, I don't need him anymore, but there is another child somewhere that this bastard had tried to molest and might have killed, but she was lucky. Arvind called her sometime back, but she doesn't want to press charges. Arvind will explain."

"Unbelievable! Tony, how is it that so much was happening in our Marsti, and we never got a whiff of anything. Some many skeletons in one closet!

Tony was trying his best to look at the case objectively, but it was all beginning to take a toll on his senses. "I have lot of work Doc, will talk to you later," said Tony, and hung up.

"Arvind, tell the judge that the investigations are ongoing, and we will need to interrogate him in the future, so that he's not let off the hook completely. We also need court permission to send his DNA samples for testing. Tell the court that we have a witness, Julie Lobo, and show them her statement. Don't ask for custody. Dr Sumanth will be here shortly."

"Sir, shall I order some breakfast for you before I leave for court? Or Eleena made me tiffin. You can have that."

"No Arvind, just ask Chhotu to send another coffee," Tony said, looking at the papers strewn across his desk, one hand massaging his forehead, other holding back a yawn.

At court, Peter was granted bail and his DNA samples were sent to Delhi with the court's permission.

His relieved parents took him home, but Peter never told anyone what Tony and Arvind had done with him that night at the police station.

22nd September
Thursday

"Arvind, come into my cabin," Tony said the following morning as soon as he entered the police station, and Arvind followed.

"I need you to come with me to the school today. Call Principal Shantiraman and ask him what would be the best time to talk to all the teachers and staff."

"Yes sir."

"I need you to make a list of all the friends and people close to the victim, and interview them, including the father."

"Which case are you talking about, sir? I thought we were talking about Sammy's case."

"We are."

"Sir, you want me to take your statement?"

"Yes," said Tony brusquely.

Looking confused but wishing to put off this particular ordeal for as long as possible, Arvind nodded, and Tony continued.

"Where is Mr and Mrs Ananth's statement?"

"They didn't say anything we didn't already know sir, on Saturday they were at the Town Hall, they went around in the afternoon and after a few rounds of golf, they lunched at the restaurant, they relaxed by the swimming pool till tea time. Some of their friends joined them soon and they came back home only at 5.30 or 6.00, they recalled," Arvind said, handing Tony the three-paged handwritten statement.

Tony scanned the statement and handed it back.

"Did you speak to Amanda?"

"She had said she will call once she is back. Or I can ask her to come back immediately."

"Not needed. Do one thing, call her and ask her if she did see anything out of ordinary or suspicious in the afternoon of 10th September, or before. We can take her official statement when she's back."

"Okay sir."

"Make the calls and get back to me. In the meantime, I am going to make the list of people to interview. Also, Arvind, you should search the victim's house, it is likely that I might have overlooked something important."

Arvind found Tony's way of speaking about Sam's case and constantly referring to her as 'victim' instead of just Sam or Samantha, strange and worrisome. It was more than impersonal; he spoke like this was someone else altogether they were discussing, someone they didn't love or even know.

They left half an hour later for the school. Amanda had not received her call so Arvind had sent her a message to call him back. Principal Shantiraman had said that the teachers would be free during lunch hour for questioning and the rest of the school staff could be interviewed any time before or after the lunch break.

Tony was taken down memory lane as soon as they reached the school. He could almost see Sam hopping down the gate, and into the imposing building like it was a funfair filled with wonders of the most amazing kind. Her friends would surround her before she reached the steps that led down the corridor into her class, talking animatedly, like happy kids do, without inhibitions. Sam would always look back and blow a kiss at Tony before disappearing into the building.

"Arvind, can you do this yourself?"

"You mean the interviews, sir? Yes. But don't you want to be there?

"I will wait in the jeep. Call me if there is anything at all. But I'd rather not go in."

"Okay sir. I understand."

Hands on the steering wheel, head bent down, Tony walked freely into the memory halls of his lovely Sam.

Arvind returned a few hours later and found Tony asleep on the wheel. Regretfully, he woke up Tony and started to brief him. He hadn't found anything useful in the case from anyone. All her teachers loved her, she was a bright child; the staff found her to be a well-mannered and respectful kid. He had even spoken to her friends with the help of her class teacher, the six-seven year olds had not been told that Sam was no more so he had to be careful. They too hadn't seen or heard anything unusual; no strangers talking to Sam or hanging out around school trying to talk to any of them.

Tony had hoped that they might find some lead at the school, but had reached another dead end.

The school peon had been waiting for Tony to wake up. He hurried towards Tony's car before he drove off, yelling, "Sir, wait!"

"Sir, I wanted to talk to you about Sam," the man said, smiling a small, shy smile.

Tony immediately got out of the car and walked around to the old man in the grey uniform.

"You knew Samantha?"

"Yes sir, and I am so sorry to hear what happened to the sweet child. Sam was an angel, sir! She was the best, most loving and kind child I have ever met, sir.

"What is your name?"

"Venkatesh, sir. I am the peon here. Been since 1999."

"How do you know my Samantha?"

"I knew Sam as all the other staff of the school did sir, as a good kid, but for this sixty-five-year-old man without any family, Sam's 'Good morning Thatha' with her endearing and open, toothy smile, lisping vocabulary, had been the best thing about his bleak days," he said embarrassed, wiping a tear off his wrinkled, tanned face. "No one ever wishes me, sir, and most ignore me, but Sam wished me every morning and evening and whenever she saw me, she grinned. I was her *thatha,* grandfather, sir. I know your pain is much more than I can understand, but I miss Sam too. I just wanted to tell you that."

"Thank you, *Thatha,*" Tony said, his voice shaking from the effort to hold back tears that threatened to break out to the surface any minute. Thinking back, he did remember that Sam had always paused briefly at the gate but Tony had never wondered why.

Not wanting to have this conversation right now, Tony casually asked Venkatesh if he had seen anything unusual around the school recently, in the past few weeks.

"No sir, just kids, and parents, and caretakers... the usual people."

After some thought, he added questioningly, "Sir, I did see someone come into the school, but he always came an hour or so after the school. Is that helpful information?"

"Who?" Tony asked, handing out the piece of paper with his number on it, thinking it must be someone to meet the principal for some school work or otherwise.

"I think his name is Mr Braganza, I am not sure. He is the owner of the new jewellery shop here in the market."

"Thomas Braganza? Are you sure?" Tony asked, alert now.

"I don't know his first name sir, I asked a couple of times but he ignored me, and just went inside, but he is the owner of the new jewellery shop, that I know, sir. But I don't think he has any kids. That's why I wondered why he came to school."

"Why didn't you stop him?"

"Sir, only a few teachers and some cleaning staff is in school after 1' o clock. And I did ask him what he was doing here, but he always just walked in without paying any attention to me."

"When was the last time you saw him? And what time?"

"I think it was a couple of days back, and before that a few weeks ago. He has come here about four or five times in the last two or three months. He usually comes around 2 or 2. 30 p.m."

"Venkatesh, think hard, and tell me if you remember anything else. Who did he meet? Where did he go in the school? Anything else you may have observed? Did you ever see who he went to meet?"

"No sir, I am sorry. From morning six to evening four, my duty is to stand at the gate. I can only leave the gate to use the toilet and nothing else. The principal is here till four o' clock sometimes, and a few teachers stay back to finish checking homework, or taking an extra class. Maybe you could check with them."

"I think I will ask the man himself first. Thank you Thatha, you have really been very helpful." Tony walked back to the driver's side.

Thomas Braganza was Constable Leslie's husband. They had both met him a few times at Town Hall during dinners and get-togethers. He came across as a very social man, too social maybe. What a childless man would be doing at school after it was closed was curious indeed.

Tony called Leslie to ask for Thomas's phone number, and when she asked why he needed it, he told her it was personal. Arvind called Thomas, asking him casually if he could drop by at the police station, and that he needed to ask him something important.

Thomas was at the police station when Arvind and Tony reached. The tall man, dressed in black T-shirt and dark blue jeans, looked more like a model than a businessman.

"How can I help you, Arvind? Have you finally decided to say your vows to Eleena? Ha! About time too!" he said with a laugh, clapping Arvind on the shoulder, following them into Tony's cabin uninvited.

"Please take a seat, Thomas," Tony said politely.

"Thank you, Tony. Do you mind ordering a coffee for me? I was at home when you called, I came without having my post-lunch green tea, but a coffee would do the job just fine. Leslie tells me the coffee here is really nice. How are you holding up, big guy?" he asked Tony in the same tone, without any sorrow in his voice.

Arvind stepped out to tell the constable to tell Chhotu for 3 coffees, and came back with a book to record his statement.

"How is the shop running?" Tony enquired casually once Arvind had taken a seat next to Thomas.

"Oh, you know how business is in small places like Marsti, just waiting for the festive season to start. But my shop has the best and latest designs, so obviously it isn't as bad as Arjan Thakkar's shop. I do plan to run him into the ground, and soon. You will see." He said the last sentence conspiratorially, and laughed out loud again.

Chhotu came with coffee shortly.

"Tell me Arvind, when is the date? I will need both of your finger sizes for the engagement bands, but you should come to the shop with Eleena to choose the rest of the jewellery. In fact, the new designs have arrived just last week. I will personally help you. And you will get the best discounts too! I like you, Arvind. Just leave everything to me."

"Has anyone from Marsti School brought anything from you yet, Thomas?" Tony asked off-handedly, sipping on his coffee.

"No. Not yet. Why? Is one of the faculty or staff having a function or wedding? I could do with tips like that, you know. I don't mind being a salesman for my own business, and I am offering the best deals all around. You should drop in too sometime, Tony."

"Oh, don't you know anyone at the school then?" Tony's voice was casual, but his eyes were watching Thomas intently, and didn't miss the momentary hesitation before he answered with a no.

"Are you sure that you don't know anyone at the school, Thomas? Are you very sure?"

"Yes! I am sure. Why would I know anyone at the school? I don't have any kids, and nor do I plan to have any," he replied haughtily, his smile replaced with a frown.

"Why have you been going to the school then?" Tony was leaning in his chair, his big arms folded in front of him, resting on the table, his dark eyes locked on Thomas's.

Thomas got up hastily, "I don't know what you are getting at, Tony. Why have I been called here?"

"Sit down, Thomas. You haven't answered my question, and I haven't even asked a difficult one yet."

"Questions regarding what? Why should I answer anything, anyway?" Thomas asked, his voice high now, his eyes stealing towards the door.

"Regarding your school visits, of course!"

"I don't know what you are talking about," he said taking a deep breath, and regaining some composure with visible effort. "And I don't need to answer anything. If you are questioning me in an official capacity, then you better have an arrest warrant or a case against me. Do you have either? I know my rights, Inspector," he said spitefully.

"I guessed not," he answered himself, when Tony didn't reply.

"I will be going now. If either of you men wish to make any purchase at 'Elegant Gold', you can drop in. Good bye," he said and started to walk off.

"What are you hiding, Thomas?" Tony asked behind him and got only a distasteful laugh in reply.

"Arvind, I need a warrant for Thomas. ASAP!" Tony said. "Now I am sure he is hiding something. But why would he go after the school closes? Was he meeting a teacher? Did any of the teachers or staff mention him at all during interviews?"

"No sir. I am surprised too. I was sure he was going to the school for some work related thing, but now, I too am convinced that he is hiding something."

Arvind called up the school principal and got the phone number for Peon Venkatesh. He called the old man and requested him to take a cab, which would be paid for, to record his statement, and started paper work for Thomas Braganza's warrant.

Dr Sumanth called Tony in the evening to tell him that the DNA reports were a match and the semen on the bed sheet belonged to Peter Sullivan. He also told him that the dust samples found in David's house were a match to those found in Sam's lungs and on her body.

Tony contemplated what this meant. Both David and Peter had alibis, so the rapist was someone else, but he was sure it was someone known to Sam and that she had been kidnapped from her own backyard.

Plus, Julie was sure she had not heard Sam shout. And he believed her, which meant Sam had definitely not been taken by force.

Peter had reached his house at around 3.30 and left by 4.00, and then Julie had checked on Sam to find her missing. That meant she was kidnapped between that time. David's guesthouse was about a thirty minute walk from Tony's house.

Sunil and his friends had seen the figure in the woods on Monday morning, 12th September at about 5.00 a.m. and on Tuesday, 13th September, close to 3.00 a.m. His daughter was alive then and if they had notified him, Sam could have been found breathing. Bruised and badly hurt, but she could have been saved. It wasn't Sunil or his friends' fault, Tony knew, and didn't blame them, but the bitterness he felt was more for his own lack of competency than their lack of judgment. If he had checked with Leslie and found out that the guesthouse hadn't been searched, he would have had a look! Had he not been so blinded with panic and pain, he would have been in his senses enough to know how to conduct the investigation.

Tony wrote the timeline in his dairy, blinded by tears of guilt and regret. He closed the dairy with a snap when he couldn't see anymore.

Leslie came hurriedly towards Tony when he was about to leave.

"Sir, sorry sir, I just wanted to ask, if you could please tell me, if it is okay with you sir, my husband sir... is everything, okay, Tony sir? He didn't say anything while leaving, but he looked angry. I asked Arvind sir, but he didn't say anything either sir. Is my Thomas in trouble, sir?" Leslie ranted on, her eyes flitting between Tony's eyes and forehead, and then at her hands, and the floor, moving from one leg to another. She kept talking till Tony put a hand on her shoulder and in shock, she stopped talking and shuddered.

"It's probably nothing, Leslie. I wish Thomas had just answered me instead of making this difficult on both of us. He will tell you anyway, so I might as well fill you in. He was seen at Marsti School, and he refused to say why he had gone there. If you can make him talk, it will be better, but if you can't convince him, I will get a warrant."

"Oh!" said Leslie, starting to cry now. "I will ask him to talk to you sir. He doesn't discuss his work with me."

She was crying profusely, tears flowing heavily from her dark eyes, a hand stealing every few seconds to wipe the tears away. "Look, maybe it is nothing. But he will have to talk to me so we can know for sure. Don't cry, my child, please calm down. This is standard procedure, and I have to follow it," Tony almost pleaded.

"Sorry sir, I will speak to him as soon as I get home. I really don't know why he would go to school, but it must be for work, sir. My Thomas is a good man, sir. I promise I am not just saying that because he is my husband, sir."

"Okay Leslie. Now don't cry and go home."

"Thank you, sir." Leslie said softly, snorting loudly.

23rd September
Friday

Arvind was at the court the whole morning and came back by 2.00 p.m. with Thomas's arrest warrant. He picked up Thomas from his house on the way to the police station. Leslie started crying seeing her husband brought in like a criminal, but didn't say anything.

Interrogation was not required as Thomas spilled the beans only after one slap. The handsome, always well-turned out, smooth talking man admitted that he was bisexual.

Thomas was having an affair with Keith Morgan, a teacher at Marsti School, and used to go there for their rendezvous.

Arvind recorded Thomas's statement; they had custody for three days, which meant Tony had no option but to keep him in one of the empty rooms of the police station.

Leslie, looking fragile for a healthy woman her size, more jumpy than she usually was, rushed to the bathroom throughout the day, at regular intervals, her bouts of gagging loud enough for everyone to hear, and feel sick themselves. By evening, Tony had had enough, and told her to take the rest of the day off.

"I am sorry Leslie. If Thomas had just answered, he wouldn't have been in this situation. I can't let him go till tomorrow, Arvind will present him to the court, and he will be home by evening. I will personally see to it that he is comfortable here tonight. Please go home and get some rest, child." Tony said, placing a large hand on her shoulders reassuringly, but she stiffened.

"Did you know about Thomas, Leslie?" Tony asked her gently as she stifled sobs.

"No sir," Leslie replied, looking at her feet, head bent down so low that Tony could only see the top of her head.

"Didn't you ever suspect anything?"

"No, sir. I never asked him about his work or where he went thereafter. Our marriage has been about both giving each other space since the beginning. Moreover, I trusted him to always be honest," she said, her voice shaking, her slumped shoulders quivering, she looked ready to faint.

Tony, concerned, requested a constable to drive Leslie home in her faded silver Wagon-R.

"Arvind, I need Principal Shantiraman's number. And come into my cabin please."

Tony called the principal at his residence, and understanding the gravity of the situation, he told Tony that he would go to the school, because all the records were in school files on his computer, and would call him back with the details. Tony waited for over an hour and was about to call the principal when he got a call. "Tony, I am emailing you Keith Morgan's file. On the second page of his resume, you will find all his personal details. Shall I come with you, Tony? This is most shocking!"

The principal was mortified at being told that one of his teachers was bisexual, and was using school grounds for illicit affairs.

"You can come if you wish, meet me outside his house."

"Okay, Tony. I have a black Honda city, number plate – 589; will wait in the car."

Tony reached forty-five minutes later but was told by the neighbour that he was out of town for a wedding and was expected the following morning.

24th September
Saturday

Tony picked up Keith Morgan early morning from the bus stop. All the clues in Sam's murder were turning to dust and this one looked no different, but Tony was a desperate man. If there was even the slightest possibility that there was more to Keith Morgan's story, then he would follow it up.

During the drive, he had questioned Tony, tried to reason with him, threatened him, begged him, and even abused him, while Tony drove quietly to the station.

At the station, Keith Morgan point blank refused to answer any personal questions. "A man's private business is so called, specifically, because it is private, Inspector Anthony. You are an educated man and to persecute a respected teacher of my standing will have dire consequences. You should let me go. I will be willing to forget your mistreatment if you just apologize," he had sermonized Tony.

"One's private life, or sexuality for that matter, is no other man's business, Keith, but you dirtied a school to satiate your sexual urges, and that makes it my business."

"Okay, so maybe I met Thomas at school, but do you have proof that the meetings were anything but innocent?"

"Yes. Thomas has given his statement, about the nature of your relationship, and has spent last night at the police station. Would you like to experience the joy of that too?"

"You can't hold me here without a warrant, Anthony. You know that. And so do I."

"That is exactly what Thomas had said too, and now I have his custody for three days. Look Keith, you are a teacher, this will malign your name more than it will cause me any trouble. Principal Shantiraman has been appraised about the matter, and the school will be taking action against you. This could potentially ruin your career. I don't care whether you are gay or bisexual or asexual! Just answer my questions and you can be on your way. In fact, if you cooperate, I will personally request the principal to not blacklist you."

"You scoundrel!" Keith spat at Tony's feet. "You can only prove anything if I talk."

"You are very close to making me lose my temper, Keith. Behave yourself unless you want to see my bad side," Tony said in a deadly voice, eyes blazing.

Why was Keith simply not admitting to the affair? Tony hadn't asked him any questions other than about his affair with Thomas. Honestly, he had no other questions; he had been literally grasping at straws, but why then was this teacher behaving as if he had something more to hide?

Keith laughed aloud, mockingly, "You want my statement. Is it? Here, write it down. I say Thomas has a grudge against me for rejecting his sexual advances, and he, with the help of his wife's friends, has made the statement to malign my image, when I threatened to out him."

"Keith—" Tony started but was interrupted.

"You prick, I will raise a campaign against you. I will make sure you never step into a police station again. Now go, and fuck yourself. I will see how long you can hold me here." Keith finished and again spat on the floor.

"What are you hiding, Keith? Not an affair, I am sure. You are behaving the way I have seen professional criminals behave when they get caught in a small matter and think they can escape, but their arrogance results in their downfall. This arrogance is ill-suited for a teacher. You are overconfident because you feel you have escaped with bigger crimes and no one will be able to persecute you for something this small. And I know I am right because you just turned ghostly pale."

Tony had learned, early on, that most in his profession used loud voice and physical power to intimidate the suspects, but the more polite you are, the more the suspect is thrown off track.

"You bastard! You know nothing. You can do nothing. Your bluff won't work on me. Nor will all these mind games. You have nothing," Keith yelled, getting up, as if to attack Tony. Tony sidestepped, lithely for a man of his size, grabbed Keith's hand and locked it behind his back with ease. Grabbing his hair, Tony half shoved, half carried the jumping and yelping teacher into the cell and locked him in.

"You asshole! You will pay for this. You can't manhandle a civilian. Just let me get out!" He spat, this time at Tony's back, as he walked away.

Tony pulled some favours and had the arrest and search warrant for Keith Morgan by that evening.

Keith Morgan's house, on the outskirts of Marsti, was a 2 BHK flat that he was renting since moving to Marsti three years ago.

Tony told Arvind to record him as he searched every room. Something about this primary school teacher made Tony want to be absolutely cautious; he felt like a slippery, struggling fish in Tony's grip who could escape, never to be seen again if Tony wasn't careful.

Tony went through the house systematically, searching every cupboard, every drawer, under the bed, in the kitchen. He searched the toilet water tanks as well as the fridge, and he searched for over two hours.

His iMac and iPad were locked, Tony put both aside to be taken in as evidence, but the locker with cash and gold wasn't.

"I had been sure he was hiding something!" Tony said finally as he sat against a table on the floor, its drawers lay at his feet. "Judge Savla will not be very happy."

"Maybe there's something in his school locker or classroom, Tony. We will check there."

Tony grunted and got up off the floor, tired, taking support of the table behind him, and suddenly it moved. "We haven't checked behind the furniture, Arvind!"

"Tony! This all is wooden furniture, not MDF or Ply! It's going to be heavy! We will have to call someone. Wait, I will see if someone in the building can help."

Making a dismissing sound, Tony got up and moved the table he had been sitting against. "Tony! You will pull a muscle, or worse. Wait, let me help you!"

"Not required. Just keep recording. Please!"

Tony went about moving the furniture, some with ease and some with difficulty, but the strong man moved the furniture himself, muscles bulging, sweat standing out at his forehead. "Wow Tony! I didn't know you worked out so much. Can you train me please?" Arvind mocked his friend, who never ceased to surprise him. And in turn was awarded with the first genuine smile.

"Yeah sure. Arvind, I will teach you to stop being your lanky, dorky self, and make you work out; and shall I climb Everest too while I am at it?"

"I am hurt, Tony. You are insulting me now!"

"Now? I always insult you, Arru," Tony used his childhood name to irritate Arvind, "you are just too slow to understand." Tony mocked and finally laughed; Arvind felt relieved.

Tony was moving the furniture while he teased Arvind. When Tony moved one of the bedside tables in the bedroom, they found a photo under it. There was a space of less than half a centimeter under the table. The picture must have fallen off unnoticed and the wind from the fan or the open windows must have blown it under.

Tony cleaned the picture that was covered in dust and dirt, and shock and anger replaced his laughter instantly. Arvind moved in to look for himself and a curse escaped him. The picture was of a child of about eight or ten, in school uniform, his knee length pants unzipped, standing in front of a urinal.

Jaw clenched, one hand balled into a tight fist, Tony made the call, "Principal, can you meet me at the school right now? Okay. Is there a master-key to teacher's lockers? Okay. Yes, collect it and meet me at the school. Yes, it is urgent and most important." He hung up and started hurriedly moving the rest of the furniture to check too. They were out of the house in fifteen minutes.

Neither spoke in the jeep. Principal Shantiraman had said the master key was with the vice principal and he would come after collecting it. They finally saw his black Honda City come down the road and he came rushing down to meet Tony and Arvind.

"What has happened, Tony? Is my school in trouble because of that fraud Keith?"

"No and yes. Did you cross-check Keith's credentials, his recommendations, his history, when you gave him the job?"

"I... don't know; it was so long ago Tony," the old man said. Kind hearted as he was, he had also been Tony's principal, and was respected and adored. But his frail memory had made most children tease him, lovingly, behind his back.

"Please think back sir, did you cross-check his degrees or his IDs or his past teaching experiences?"

"It was almost three years back, Tony. I really don't remember. It is the standard procedure, so I must have. But I can't be sure as I don't recollect it."

Principal opened the school main gate and the main door and the trio walked down the school corridor, the principal switching a light here and there. Tony went straight into the boy's toilet, switched on all the lights, and an astonished principal followed. Tony and Arvind kept looking at a picture and up at the toilet walls.

"There!" Tony said finally and got up on the toilet platform, tapping the wall with his knuckles, feeling everywhere with his palms, he was about to tell Arvind that he wanted to remove the tube light to check behind it when he saw a wire poking out of one side. It looked too thin for a standard electric wire. Carefully, Tony picked the wire and followed it and found the battery, and the other end was attached to a screw. Delicately, Tony removed the whole unit and got down.

"What is this Tony?" Principal Shantiraman asked.

"It's a spy camera, sir. Keith Morgan was filming children here."

Principal Shantiraman was about to collapsc when Tony held him and took him outside with the help of Arvind.

"Wait here, Arvind! I want to check the girls' toilet, his locker and classroom too."

Tony came back, looking relieved that there was no camera in the girls' toilet. He hadn't found anything of concern in the locker room or his class room either.

Arvind called a software engineer to unlock the phone and laptop.

Tony went into the cell holding Keith Morgan, picked him up, almost off his feet, and punched him hard in the stomach. His teeth clicked together hard with the force of the blow and blood spurted out of his gums and onto the floor.

"You fucking bastard! I want to kill you right now!" Tony let go of Keith's collar and he piled on the floor like a rag doll. Trying to control himself, Tony tried breathing in and out, as he felt the rage overclouding his senses.

"You will rot in a dark cell for a long time, you sick asshole! I will see to it that you do! How I wish I could kill you!" Tony kicked the balled up man in his stomach and walked out, locking the cell behind him.

25th September
Sunday

The teachers and staff of Marsti School came to the police station by afternoon. Tony had called Principal Shantiraman to check how he was and also get the numbers of all the staff members and teachers.

The photos and videos on Keith's laptop and phone were enough to convict him. Arvind spent the day interviewing the teachers to get more information on Keith and his behaviour while Tony checked his records. The school staff and teachers had only good to say about Keith, while his records were found to be completely forged.

Tony was on the phone when Arvind stepped in with the statements of the two teachers. "Keith Morgan has air tight alibis for the day of Sam's kidnapping, Tony," he said looking surprised. "It can be easily verified. After school on that Saturday, some of the teachers had stayed back to correct the quarterly school test papers for primary classes. They were at school till 5.00 in the evening and then one of them had suggested that they stop over for a few beers at David's bar. I have already told the manager to send over the CCTV footage to verify this and Principal Shantiraman will be sending the school CCTV recordings too. Keith Morgan was so drunk by 8.00 p.m. that he could hardly walk. One of the teachers took him home and he spent till next evening, which is Sunday evening, at that teacher's house. This teacher's wife has been called to give a statement too, and they have a five-year-old son, who Keith had spent the afternoon watching TV with. I don't know if he should be questioned, sir."

"Maybe for some reason the victim went into the woods and got lost and our search team missed her and after leaving from this teacher's house, Keith Morgan went into the woods himself and found the victim."

"But, sir..." Arvind started to say doubtfully.

"I know it looks unlikely, but it's not implausible. And who, if not Keith Morgan?" Tony knew what he was saying was impossible. The chances of him and over a hundred people searching for Sam and not finding her, and Keith Morgan just stumbling upon her, were next to nil, but this was their last lead in the case. "The man is a pedophile! What are the chances that more than one monster is in Marsti at the moment?"

"That is a petrifying thought, Tony. Honestly. The idea of a single man like Keith Morgan is scary enough, but to think of another such heinous villain walking amongst us is chilling!"

"Tomorrow we have to take him to the court. I plan to ask for custody of one week to fifteen days. Oh! And don't call the teacher's son or anything. But do talk to this teacher and his wife and ask them to have a talk with their son, to check if Keith Morgan did anything inappropriate.

26th September
Monday

Arvind took Keith to the court where custody was granted till 3rd October 2016. Thereafter, Keith Morgan was to be transferred to Chennai Central Jail for further proceedings.

On the way back, Arvind got a call from Amanda. Parking his jeep on the side of the highway, he answered his mobile phone. She said that she had tried calling Tony but hadn't been able to reach him.

"I will be returning this evening, Arvind. Can you please tell me why you had wanted to see me?" Amanda asked.

"Ma'am, we need your statement in an ongoing investigation. Is it possible for you to come to the police station tomorrow morning at 9.00 a.m.?" Arvind asked, formally.

"Investigation? Have I been robbed!?" she asked, her usually, deliberately, husky voice hoarse with fear.

"No, you have not been robbed. It is a different case, but I don't have permission to divulge the information on phone. You will have to come down to the police station, ma'am. It will not take too much time. It's more procedural formality than anything else."

"Tell me what has happened at least! You know me, Arvind, you can trust me."

Arvind knew he couldn't trust Amanda at all. "Ma'am, is 9.00 a.m. tomorrow morning suitable for you?" Tony had told Arvind to ask Amanda on the phone if she had seen anything, but the woman's phone had been continuously unreachable, and now she was coming back herself, so they could directly record her statement. "Or, you could come in today between 5.00 and 7.00 p.m. and we could talk."

"Oh... I think I could come in by sixish, if that's okay?"

Tony didn't take his eyes off the file that lay in front of him as Arvind entered and took a seat across the table.

"Did we get a couple of days in custody at least?" Tony said, looking at Arvind now.

"We have him till the 3rd of October. Give me a few hours with him, Tony. I will make him sing like a canary."

"You will get more than a few hours, don't worry."

"Actually I am worried a little, Tony. We still haven't got anything to tie Keith to Sam's murder. I wonder what we are missing! If only there was some clue," Arvind stopped talking, a veil of sadness had fallen on Tony's eyes again at the mention of Sam, he realized regretfully. "I am sorry sir."

"Don't be sorry, Arvind. I have to deal with this all my life. I can't break down at the mere mention of her name. Sam is always on my mind, but I have to stop taking out the anger on everyone around me," Tony said soberly.

"Arvind, I also want to meet and apologize to Mrs Krishnan for my behaviour at the funeral. I will call and ask to meet her soon."

"And that reminds me, Amanda called back finally, she is coming down to the police station around 6.00 p.m. today."

"That's good," Tony said and got up from his seat, unbuckling his uniform belt "Now, shall we go see Mr Keith Morgan, and teach him a few things for a change?" Tony smiled, an angry, sad smile.

Keith's yells were heard through the police station for the next hour till a constable interrupted to tell them Amanda D'silva was waiting at Arvind's desk.

In a white collared silk shirt, buttons at the throat left open to give a peak at her big silicon breast, an elegant, body hugging black skirt that rode up just high enough above her knees to show her shapely thighs, black stilettoes complimenting the expensive outfit, Amanda D'silva looked dressed for a lavish party rather than the police station.

"Hi darling," she said getting up from her chair and walking towards Tony. She hugged him, "I just heard what happened." Tony took a step to a side to walk out of her arms. Embarrassed, he walked straight to Arvind's table and took a chair. Arvind sat in his own.

Amanda walked to Tony's chair and kneeled, "Oh babe, I am so sorry for your loss." Taking his hand in her own, she held it at her breast, "I can understand what you are going through. I am with you. Don't feel alone."

"I am fine Amanda, don't worry. Take a seat, please."

"Oh, of course," said Amanda as if just registering her surroundings. Tony got up and went to stand behind Arvind's desk, next to his chair.

Barely able to control his laugh, Arvind coughed, to hide the escaped giggle. He had never seen Tony look scared of anyone, but he always looked nervous around Amanda. And rightly so.

She had that seductive and dangerous, dominatrix air about her, which said she was more than capable of bringing out her whip any minute.

Clearing his throat, "Arvind, take Amanda's statement. I have a few calls to make," said Tony and walked towards his cabin.

"I will see you after this, Tony. I will need a lift back home. You see, I was too tired from the journey to drive, so I took a cab down here," she said slowly, in her husky voice.

"I am sorry Amanda, I havc to work till late tonight," Tony said at the door. "I will arrange a cab or one of the constables can drop you on their way for evening patrol.

Amanda sighed "Okay", and another giggle escaped Arvind's lips.

Clearing his throat loudly, "Ma'am, were you home on Saturday, the 10th of September?" Arvind started.

They got nothing out of Amanda. She had been in her room at the back of the house, packing, all afternoon.

27th September
Tuesday

Tony reached the police station with Arvind and interrogated Keith Morgan again. The man still refused to speak. Tony was getting frustrated now. Keith was their last lead. Every other clue had ended in nothing. He realized that if Keith Morgan was not the killer, then the killer was still roaming free. Free to destroy another family. Free to hurt another child.

Tony sent a constable to bring him a bottle of Teacher's from David's bar. The constable told the manager that Tony had ordered him to bring the alcohol, who in turn called David. David, without missing a beat, called Mrs Krishnan to tell her that Tony was drinking on duty, but didn't find her in office.

"Tony, maybe you should go home. It's 8.30. I can drop you on the way," Arvind said. He had wanted to stop Tony when he had ordered the whiskey, but couldn't.

"Arvind, come in." Tony slurred. "Do you think I am missing something?"

"Why do you ask sir?" Arvind asked clueless.

"I don't think Keith Morgan is a killer. Though the bastard refuses to talk, I know a killer when I see one. This guy is a piece of shit, but there is no reason to not believe the teachers who say they were with him. But then, who is my Sam's murderer?"

"Sir, let me take you home," Arvind said after a minute. He had been thinking the same – Keith Morgan was undoubtedly a pedophile, but his dirty twisted mind was into boys. They had found child porn and pictures of boys on his laptop, but nothing to point towards his link to Sam's murder.

"I am going to make that asshole talk out of his asshole today. You go on," Tony said getting up from his chair and stumbled out. After a moment's consideration, Arvind followed him, to make sure that Tony didn't kill Keith Morgan in his cell.

After two days of beating but refusing to talk, Keith Morgan finally broke when Tony broke his toe in anger. Begging to be taken to a doctor, wailing in pain, he finally started to talk and the mysteries about the man's life were revealed.

Kieth Morgan was in fact Keith Periera. A 12th fail from Mangalore. He had raped two boys before and had escaped to Chennai when he was about to get caught. One of the victims had been his own nephew. He had finally fled Chennai when the third boy had complained to his parents.

He confessed to selling the recordings from school to some pimp for money.

"How did you murder my Sam?" Tony asked suddenly. He sat in one corner of the cell after breaking Keith's toe, drinking, while Arvind asked questions.

Surprised, the sub inspector and the malefactor both looked at Tony. He got up and walked over to the man sitting in the chair, his mouth red with blood, his cheeks swollen, his left leg resting in an awkward position to lessen the pain. "I asked you something, you dirt sack! How did you murder my Sam!?"

"Tony..." Arvind started to say something, but Tony had hit the man in the stomach hard enough for him to fall off the chair and he started gagging. Picking him up holding his dirty shirt collar, Tony hit him in his sides again, and the man with one heavy breath lost consciousness completely. Arvind rushed out of his own chair and held Tony's hand from hitting the man again. "You will kill him, Tony. Stop it!"

Tony turned, hand raised to strike Arvind, who looked on, taken aback at the viciousness in him. After a thought, the look of evil went out of Tony's eyes, to be replaced by one of disgust. Casting aside the 90 kg man like he was made of stuffed cotton, Tony stormed out of the cell.

Arvind called the constable and checked Keith's breathing. Putting him on the bedding laid out on the floor, Arvind asked the constable to sit outside the cell and keep checking on Keith every ten minutes and to call him if there was any problem or if he seemed ill.

"What are you doing Tony?" Arvind shouted entering Tony's room.

Tony sat on his desk. Head held in both hands. "I am losing my mind, Arvind. This is another dead end." He replied, regretfully.

"That doesn't give you the right to kill someone!" Arvind was scared for Tony.

"Let me drop you home, Tony. We will talk tomorrow. And we will find Sam's murderer. I promise. Just stop drinking yourself to your own destruction," Arvind said pleading.

30th September
Friday

Next day, Tony went to work after a sleepless night, drunk, in a cab at 7.00 a.m. He couldn't stay at home. He heard Sam's cries even while awake now. At first, in the drunken stupor, he thought her cries were coming from inside the house but after an hour of rushing from one room to another and then out into the woods, calling out her name, he had realized that he was really losing his mind.

When Arvind came in and looked into his cabin, he found Tony napping at his desk, a bottle of whiskey lying at his hand. Arvind picked up the bottle and hid it in his own desk drawer.

"Arvind, get me the guest list of the hotels in Marsti and all the CCTV footage, too. There are no CCTV cameras installed on my street, but there are plenty inside and outside all the hotels. I want them as soon as possible. If they refuse to release them, let me know." Tony ordered, in a rude manner, which was unlike him.

"Sir, may I ask why we need this footage?"

"No! You may not! Just do as you are told!"

Arvind stood there looking at the man who looked like his boss and friend, but wasn't behaving like him at all. Tony looked up finally.

"Arvind, I am sorry. I find it more and more difficult to keep myself in check. Please call the hotels and ask them for the footage and guest-list for 10th September. It is far-fetched, but the only theory left is that the killer was a tourist?"

"Sir, that's not too far-fetched! In fact, that's probably why we haven't found the guy yet! Some trekker may have found her like the children who found her body. I will get to it right away," Arvind said breathlessly.

Tony sat impassive. He knew it was most unlikely because for a tourist to kidnap a child from her own house, unseen, take her to the only abandoned building in town, clean up well enough to erase every finger print, throw the body back in the woods instead of leaving it in the guesthouse, meant that this was all planned. This couldn't have been done by an outsider. And most importantly, and this is what scared him the most, Sam had gone with the killer herself. This meant it was not only someone local, but someone Sam knew and trusted. Someone he himself must know.

Outside, from his desk, Arvind called the manager of Noble Hotel but he refused to give any information without a warrant. "That girl, Kavitha, I gave you the phone number of, she called here, yes, and threatened the hotel with legal action for releasing her information. I thought it was police's prerogative to issue unnecessary threats!" he laughed shortly. "Sorry Arvind, I have been told to not release any information about guests by our lawyer."

Arvind knew Tony was not in the right frame of mind and decided to call Mrs Krishnan; she liked Tony well enough and hopefully had forgiven his rude behaviour. The town mayor agreed to call the hotel owners and said her secretary will call him back in sometime. In half an hour Arvind got a call from Mrs Krishnan's secretary and was told that by evening someone from the hotels would drop the CCTV footages and records for the 10th of September at the police station.

1st October
Saturday

Mrs Krishnan had herself called the hotel owners at Arvind's request and asked them to release the hotel records and CCTV footage. The owners had done as asked, but came to see her and expressed their displeasure at such an unlawful demand.

Mrs Krishnan knew this was not the procedure, but Tony was a desperate father and she had tried her best to explain the same to them. Out of understanding, respect, or fear of getting in the bad books of the town mayor, they had agreed to cooperate with Tony in the investigation.

She had decided to have a word with Tony even before David showed up soon after. He whined about police torture and brutality, unlawfully being detained, and said he planned to file an official complaint with the commissioner, and apprise him about Tony's new practice of drinking on duty.

Mrs Krishnan was disturbed about the last bit. She had heard stories of Tony being drunk all the time, on and off duty.

In a small town like Marsti, everyone had a business knowing another's business.

She disliked David the most in town. His bar served alcohol to teenagers, it was close to college and kids had made it their new hangout, druggies and prostitutes from out of town were regulars there, and her countless efforts to shut the place down had failed.

"Okay David. Tony is much respected and has many friends in this town, including me. Did you know that?"

"Yes ma'am, but..."

"I suggest you pay more attention on your bar than getting into legal hassles with upright citizens, or law personnel in town. You wouldn't want the list of your enemies to increase now. Would you?" she asked with concern and David's face turned a hideous tomato red.

"No, Madam Mayor," he said through clenched teeth and left.

2nd October
Sunday

Tony had stayed back at the police station, reviewing the guest-list. Sometime during the night he had slept and was woken up when Arvind came in the morning with coffee and breakfast, which he refused. When Arvind came back sometime around noon to tell him that Mrs Krishnan was there to see him, he was aghast to see Tony drinking again.

"Ma'am, Tony sir has to go out for a round up, could you come back in the evening?" he had told Mrs Krishnan, apologetically, knowing she would not go without seeing Tony.

Mrs Krishnan strode into Tony's cabin to see him putting away the bottle of whiskey, but the room stank of alcohol and cigarettes. Trying to smile pleasantly, her liking for Tony stronger than her hate for drunks since her husband had passed away due to liver failure. She said hello and took a seat.

"How are you, Tony? Did you receive the CCTV footage that you wanted?"

"Yes ma'am. Arvind told me that you had to speak to them to release it. I owe you thanks, and sorry," Tony said steadily but his eyes were bloodshot.

"Why sorry, Tony?" she quizzed.

"Sorry for my ill behaviour at the funeral. I know you were only trying to help, and I behaved most discourteously. I meant to call on you personally to apologies, but work has delayed me. Please forgive me for that day, Mrs Krishnan."

"No apology needed. I understood then and I understand now. And to you, I am Madhu Akka, Tony," she said, her heart going out to the man. She had known Tony as the most honest and decent police officer Marsti had seen. She had seen him as a loving husband and a devoted father. She had seen him as a fun-loving, intelligent man and a trustworthy friend. But now, she only saw the hallow shell of misery that he had become.

"Thank you, ma'am, you are very kind. And thank you again for your help," he said, trying to smile, but failing.

He rang the bell on his desk and asked the constable to send for two coffees.

"Tony, I have come here for a particular reason. I hope you will not take it otherwise, but I have a suggestion, unsolicited, to make." Tony looked on politely as Mrs Krishnan continued, "but a question first and I ask as an elder sister. Not the Mayor."

Tony nodded and she asked, "Were you drinking when I came in?"

"Yes ma'am," Tony replied, emotionlessly.

"Don't you think it is wrong to be drinking on duty?

"Yes ma'am."

"Tony, I tried to tell you that day at the funeral but it was possibly the wrong place and time to say anything, but I know your pain is great. What happened to Sam, if it happened, God forbid," she crossed herself, "to my Shwetambari, I would probably die."

Tony was trying his best to not think about what exactly had happened to Sam but the visions were starting again. Tony shut his eyes, wishing the vision and voices faded away, but they were growing vivid and loud.

"I know it must be difficult to go back to the same house where Sam once played. I can't imagine what kind of animal would do that to a little child. It's unbelievable!" she was talking softly, feeling the father's pain.

"I know that no words can lessen the pain or comfort you, Tony, but life must go on. And..." her voice completely drowned in Sam's shouts for help echoing in Tony's head. Tony, with his eyes closed could see her crying out for help while a dark man threw soil on her, her mouth was filling up with mud and she was choking. He was trying to run towards Sam or wake up from this nightmare, but he was immovable! He was trying to screech at the man to scare him away, but his voice failed. Soon, his daughter was buried alive in the grave. The man turned then, dressed in black, his face hidden under his black cloak, he pointed at Tony and started laughing. The laugh was rising and falling in his head like excruciating pain. Tony couldn't take it anymore and suddenly jerked awake.

"Shut up!" yelled Tony.

Mrs Krishnan sat shocked.

"Stop laughing, you bastard! I will kill you!" His open eyes looked around the room searching for the cloaked man.

"Tony! What..."

"Shut up! I said *shut up*!"

"Don't say another word!" he shouted loudly to no one.

"Tony, I didn't mean to aggravate your pain. I just wanted to suggest..."

"Shut up! Stop laughing! I will kill you!" he said banging his hands hard on the table, not seeing Mrs Krishnan anymore, but trying to find the laughing man.

"Ma'am, you please come with me," Arvind rushed over to Mrs Krishnan. Hands on her arms, he led her out of the room, looking over his shoulder at Tony as if he would attack any minute.

Arvind escorted Mrs Krishnan to her car and the stunned pale woman told her driver to drive home.

Tony's voice could be heard till the police station gate.

Mrs Krishnan asked the driver to stop some distance away and leave her alone for some time. Unable to hold back anymore, the fifty-year-old of stern looks but a kind heart broke down; and she cried, big sobs shaking her large frame.

A drunken police officer is not only useless, but also dangerous. And as the mayor of Marsti, she had to take some steps to help the situation.

When her sobs subsided, she took a sip of water from the mineral water bottle and took her phone out. After another minute, she called the police commissioner.

4th October
Tuesday

Arvind arrived at Tony's house in the evening to find the main door ajar, and Tony passed out on the sofa. The house was a mess – alcohol bottles littering every table, burned out or extinguished cigarette butts spread over every piece of furniture and stubbed in dirty dishes.

Tony was asked to go on a paid leave with immediate effect the previous morning and the news had spread like wildfire in Marsti.

Arvind started picking up the beer and whiskey bottles and the dirty plates to put them in the kitchen. He opened the fridge to get a bottle of water and saw Tupperware containers filled with food stacked one on top of the other and half a dozen more beer bottles.

"Hey, wake up bro!"

Tony looked around opening his eyes slowly and smiled sorrowfully when he saw the efforts Arvind had employed to make the house look habitable.

"Hi, how are you? When did you come?" Tony asked, rubbing his head automatically.

"Aren't you going to ask me how I got in?"

"No. I left the door open. Anyone could have got in."

"Why?" Arvind was staggered.

"Hoping Sam's murderer would come in to finish the job," he said morosely.

"Tony, if you want to start yelling at me too, go ahead! But I have to tell you this. You have to get a grip, man! I think what Mrs Krishnan did was right."

Tony raised an eyebrow, smiling, as Arvind continued, "Yes. I also think you behaved like a madman that day and the poor old woman, thankfully, didn't have a heart attack, but she was scared for her life!"

Without saying a word, he got up, looking around for his whiskey bottle that Arvind had put in the kitchen. Tony fetched it and took a sip, neat, from the bottle and collapsed heavily on the sofa again.

"Tony, you need to hear this."

"No, I don't," he said taking another sip of whiskey.

"But you are going to. Are you going to start shouting or are you going to simply hit me? Go ahead. But someone has to tell you this and I should have long back."

"Please Arvind..." Tony pleaded and that stopped Arvind's angry tirade. He looked empathetically at his brother, his friend, and his eyes misted over. The strong, confident, courageous man he knew was replaced by this sorry figure with slumped shoulders, baggy eyes and smelly clothes.

"Tony, please. *Anna,* you have to get a hold of yourself, for Angela and Sam's sake, if not your own."

"Please don't talk about Sam, Arvind. I beg of you."

"I won't, Tony. But are you going to let her killer get away with it?"

"*No!*" Tony answered vociferously.

"Then you have to live and be in your senses."

"I don't know how to live anymore, Arvind. I feel lost. Every lead, every clue, everything has ended into nothing." He took another swing at the bottle in his hand.

"Tony, please, you can't give up till you have brought the bastard to book. In fact, once you find him, hand him over to me. I will serve him what he deserves. We will punish the motherfucker! Together, we will find him and kill him. Just don't waste away before we do, though. Please."

Speechless, Tony, his eyes unblinking, put his head back on the sofa and stared at the ceiling.

"Keith Morgan has been sent to Chennai Jail. Once we file the charge sheet, his trail will start."

"That's some good news," he said apathetically.

"How are you sleeping since Sam, Tony?" Tony had been losing weight.

"Poorly." Came the impassive reply and he took another sip, reached into his pocket and brought out the cigarette packet. "Is there a lighter on that table behind you?" he asked.

"Tony, do you mind if I stay over for a few days?" Arvind asked without looking for the lighter on the table behind him.

"Why?" he asked in the same emotionless tone.

"Can I?"

Tony simply shrugged his shoulders and started looking around for his lighter.

Arvind went into the kitchen to check what could be salvaged for dinner from the food and came back with a plate of biryani.

"Who is the chef?" Arvind asked when he sat down, handing Tony his plate who started picking at it disinterested, looking at Arvind in confusion. "Who has been so kind to bring all the food that is rotting in your fridge?" he elaborated.

"Mrs Ananth brings food. Sometimes Amanda too."

"Tony, the new officer will take charge from tomorrow itself. Should I speak to Mrs Krishnan? I could request her to talk to the commissioner? I could convince her. She still likes you. You know that. Right?"

"No Arvind. I don't need you to beg anyone, and I don't care who likes me or doesn't."

Arvind stayed that night and for the next week. Tony spent his nights reading Sam's case files that he had photocopied before leaving the office and days drinking, and in between, he wandered in the woods. Sometimes crying, sometimes calling out Sam's name.

Arvind was getting worried and asked Eleena to drop in one day. Tony had refused to seek medical help or counselling for his emotional trauma, which he said was not trauma but failure, or for his continual weight loss.

Eleena came and tried talking to Tony, casually, but his response was the same that Arvind got these days – cold, curt, detached. On the way to drop her home, Eleena told Arvind that she was more worried about Tony's mental health than physical.

"In extreme cases, depression due to loss can sometimes lead a person to want to give up on everything, even themselves. Didn't you see how blank he was throughout the evening? He didn't smile even once! His face was devoid of any emotions. He needs to find the will to live again, Arvind."

Feeling helpless himself, Arvind dropped Eleena and went back to find Tony drinking, staring at the black TV screen. He didn't notice when Arvind came in, or sat across him, or when he put a blanket around him. Arvind wondered how he could convince Tony to see a psychiatrist.

16th October
Sunday evening

Arvind went to the barbershop and realized that everyone in town was starting to call Tony mad or suggesting that he was losing his marbles. He was being called a stalker, a psycho, a woman-beater and so on.

"... That was some sight. Drooling, he was wearing soiled clothes!" someone said.

Arvind came back without a haircut to find Tony ambling away in the backyard of his house.

He called his uncle, but was told that he was not home and would be back the next day. A retired psychiatrist from a reputed hospital in Mumbai, his maternal uncle had decided to spend the final years of his life at his birth place, Pondicherry. Arvind left a message to be called back as soon as he was back.

That day at work, Arvind was so busy that he didn't get a chance to call and check up on Tony. He was worried when Tony didn't answer in the evening. When he reached home, he saw Tony sitting in front of the blank TV screen.

"Tony! Why didn't you answer the phone!? I have been calling for an hour!"

"Sorry."

"What were you doing?"

"Nothing."

"You need to do something, Tony!"

"What?" he asked blankly and Arvind felt a weight drop in his heart and another lift in his brain. He knew what Tony needed. Tony needed to do something. Anything that kept his mind occupied. Anything to keep him occupied.

"I know what! Tony, get up and come here." Arvind said, leading Tony to the sofa where he fell, lifelessly.

"Tony, I know how we can find a lead into Sam's murder." Arvind waited for a response and got one immediately. At the mention of Sam's name, Tony became alert and Arvind realized what a mistake he had been making by avoiding talking about Sam. Tony's daughter was his only reason to live and after her, finding her killer had occupied Tony's mind, but when he thought he wouldn't find the killer, that he had exhausted all leads, he had lost hope.

"Tony, what if we have missed some clue because we didn't look at the case from a third person perspective?" Tony gave him a quizzical look, but Arvind was feeling happy. This was the first conversation since suspension that Tony had taken any interest in.

"There have been so many rapes and murders, what if in one of the other case files, there is a clue to our killer?"

"I don't understand, Arvind," Tony said, his voice low, hoarse, and rusty.

"What I mean is, we should see other case files of South India, and across India, too. Similar cases have been solved before and maybe the procedure followed in other cases will give us a new viewpoint into our case!"

Slowly, understanding dawned upon Tony and his face looked brighter, somehow.

"Yes! That's a brilliant idea, Arvind! Looking at other cases might give us a new angle into our Sam's case. Yes, that's a good idea."

"Okay. So you go and take a shower, I will make dinner and we will start immediately.

"Okay Arvind," Tony said excitedly and walked into the bathroom.

Arvind cried silently, exultant at the hope of saving his brother.

17th October
Monday

Tony woke up around 1.00 p.m.

Arvind had left early for the police station leaving a note for Tony, to eat and not drink much, and that there was bacon and boiled eggs in the oven.

Tony showered, ate, and started searching on Google. He began researching the cases he had shortlisted last night. Reading every available detail in newspapers, he spent the day on his laptop. And when Arvind came, he realized it was after dark.

He was feeling a sense of purpose again. Arvind and Tony had dinner discussing the cases, and after washing the dishes, he made coffee and resumed the research while Arvind retired.

Tony slept in a few hours, tired, without alcohol, but his sleep was disturbed by the same dreams again. He woke up sometime during the night, made himself a drink and continued reading till the morning.

Each case reminded him of Sam, but his rediscovered resolve to find the killer was stronger than before. Tony kept working systematically, and when he read about any case similar to Sam's, he went back to the date of the crime and started reading every article in chronological order.

There were so many cases. Each day a new rape case or more, and each more gruesome than the last.

Over the next few days, Tony went through many cases. On the 19th October, he chanced upon a case of a rapist, Garry Damascus, who was caught fourteen years back.

Tony read about him, and was shocked to learn that he had raped his own niece, who was almost as young as Sam. Thankfully he was caught and sentenced to jail on his niece's statement in the court, but that had come at the cost of another child's life that he had raped, and murdered in 2002. Tony, reading the statement of the girl in the newspaper felt his heart going out for the child.

Her name was withheld in the articles. It said she was raped repeatedly by her uncle since she was eight years old. The girl had somehow escaped the misery her life had become when she started college and went to stay in the hostel. The perpetrator was a police officer himself, with a service record of twenty years in Chennai police force, and had retired in 2000. A year later, he had raped and murdered a five-year-old, and kept her body hidden in his house for weeks. The articles didn't say much about the child who was his unfortunate niece, but a few articles dated around the time that Garry was caught, described the way the body of the other girl was found.

The child had been raped, mutilated, cut with sharp

objects, bitten, and then stuffed in a gunny bag and kept in his own bedroom cupboard. It had been the neighbours who had discovered the source of the foul smell and alerted the police.

The coincidence of similarities between the ways that the killers had brutally murdered the victims alerted Tony, but it said that Garry Damascus was sentenced to life imprisonment.

He tried reading other cases but his mind kept going back to the teen child whose name the newspapers had withheld. What must have become of her? Was she okay now? He read and reread the Garry Damascus case articles, over and over again, wondering how two murders set fifteen years apart could be so analogous.

After much thought and contemplation, Tony decided that there were far too many similarities in the cases to ignore and he had to read the police files.

He dialled Inspector Pervez Sheikh, his batch mate at the police training academy. When the phone went unanswered, he redialled and looked at his wrist watch. It was 12.15 a.m. As he was about to disconnect the call, he heard him.

"Hello?" said a sleepy gruff voice.

"Hello, Pervez? It's Anthony George from Marsti."

"Tony? Why are you calling at this time?"

"I need some information about a case. It's important and urgent. Call me once you wake up."

"Okay." Came the reply and the call was disconnected.

20th October
Thursday, 11.00 a.m.

Around 11.00 a.m. Pervez Sheikh called Tony.

"Hey Anna, how are you?"

"I am good Pervez Anna. How is life treating you?"

"Good. What can I do for you?"

"Pervez, I need a case file. It's from 2002. Can you arrange it?"

"You mean police case file? Chennai case?"

"Yes."

"Of course not! That's illegal, Tony. You know that."

"Yes, but could you try? It's important, Pervez. Very important!"

"Which case and why is it important?"

Tony had no choice but to explain to Pervez what had happened to Sam, how the cases were similar, and why he wanted to see the Garry Damascus files. Pervez, horrified, sad for Tony and Sam, agreed and said he would check and get back to Tony as soon as he had something.

Tony waited all day, anxious to hear from Pervez, reading other cases online, but his mind kept going back to this one particular case. Arvind came home to find Tony pacing the house. Worried, he asked what was wrong, but got no reply.

Next morning, 21st October 2016, Pervez called Tony to say that the files could be arranged by the next day, but couldn't be sent by email or post.

"These are confidential police files and this particular case was much publicized because it involved a police officer. The best that I can do is, get the photocopy of the files, but you will have to come here to collect them yourself. This could cost me my job if it got out, Tony. I hope you know that." Tony understood the risks involved and agreed immediately.

"I can leave on the last bus from Marsti, it reaches Chennai around 6-7 a.m. and return on the next bus. Where should I collect the files from?"

"I will come to the bus station. I will collect and photocopy the files once the case officer has it. But there is a condition, Tony." Tony knew that going against the system even for something as small as reading closed files could cost an officer his job and more.

"What?" Tony asked.

"You cannot go back the same day. In fact, you can't go back for a couple of days."

"Why?"

"There are two reasons. One is that the officer has warned that the files not be given to anyone else."

"I understand that. I suppose I could stay in some hotel for a couple of days. Yes. Pervez, don't worry. I will read the files and give them back to you."

"Good that you have no problem with reading the files here. Second reason is more of a complaint than a reason."

"Complaint? Against whom?"

"You! You never came to my wedding. Your own wedding was a court affair. You haven't even met my kids! I have two little girls. Did you know? You have to stay for a few days at my house."

"Please Pervez, not this time. Next time I will definitely stay with you, brother. But..."

"No but! If you don't stay over for two days at least, I will not get the files for you. I had to use all my contacts and the goodwill of years of my service to find that officer and convince him! I am jeopardizing my career for you, and you cannot stay with your own nieces for a few days!?" Pervez finished in a huff and Tony started laughing. He hadn't laughed so openly for weeks, he realized, and when the guilt of happiness hit him, he choked. Tears in his eyes, he agreed to stay with Pervez Sheikh for a couple of days and thanked him.

22nd October
Saturday

Tony told Arvind that evening that he wanted to investigate a case, and hence was travelling to Chennai. Arvind was relived just to see Tony out and about. He dropped Tony to the bus station and on the way back picked up Eleena for dinner.

The tables were occupied and they decided to take a drink and wait by the pool side. Arvind saw Leslie sitting on one of the tables, alone. Her husband Thomas was talking to a group of people animatedly.

His sexual orientation hadn't become public. All anyone knew was that Tony had questioned him. Thomas behaved indignantly about the whole episode and Arvind had heard some of the stories he was spreading around about his own bravery, and Tony being afraid when Thomas had told him of his connections. Arvind didn't know whether to laugh at Thomas's claims or to call his bluff, but he had thought about beating the loud mouth into telling the truth a couple of times. The only reason he had kept quiet was Leslie. She was a colleague and a nice woman, if a little irritatingly apologetic, and clumsy.

There were no tables free, so Arvind and Eleena went over to Leslie and asked if they could sit at her table for some time. Awkwardly smiling, Leslie nodded.

"Can I order you a drink, Leslie?" Arvind asked.

"Water please. I couldn't get the attention of the waiter." He couldn't understand the odd couple that Leslie and Thomas made. Arvind ordered beers for himself and Eleena, and water and a watermelon juice for Leslie.

Arvind resumed talking to Eleena about the change that had come about in Tony in just a couple of days.

"I can't believe this. The other day when I saw him, he wouldn't even talk. But are you sure he will be okay travelling by himself?" Eleena asked, concerned.

The waiter came with their drinks, served and left.

"Of course. That's what I have been telling you; he looked almost like the old Tony. Not the Tony when Angela was alive, or the one he had become when Sam was with us, but the Tony after she passed away. It's definitely an improvement on the comatose like state he had been in for the last couple of weeks."

"Where is he travelling to?" Leslie asked, surprising Arvind and Eleena. They had forgotten she was at the table.

"Tony left for Chennai sometime back," Arvind answered with a smile.

"Why Chennai? How is he now?" Leslie asked concerned.

"He is researching some old case. I don't know exactly. Like I was telling El, after being suspended, he had become a robot. Completely lifeless. But he is better now."

"I still can't believe that all this has happened in our Marsti. Arvind, she looked like my own little daughter." Eleena said forlornly. Arvind put a hand over hers.

"What old case and why?"

"I really don't know. He just said he had to leave and he was meeting his old batch mate in Chennai, Inspector Pervez Sheikh," he replied to Leslie and turned to Eleena, trying to change her train of thoughts, and change the subject, since she always got sad at the subject of her daughter. "You know El, Sheikh sir was my senior at the academy. I had heard so many stories about him and Tony sir! They were quite a pair of trouble makers. They didn't even spare the faculty!" Arvind laughed at the memories.

He continued fondly, addressing both the women, "I have always looked up to Anthony sir since school. He is one of the reasons I decided to join the force. He was always this hero for all his juniors and leader to his classmates and some seniors too. Hah! I remember this one time, it was teacher's day and all the—" Arvind was startled as Leslie dropped her glass of juice

"Hey! Leslie, are you okay?"

Leslie was looking blank with fear. "Leslie," he said kneeling down. "Don't worry. It's just a glass."

"I am sorry. I am so sorry," she started apologizing again. Arvind felt pity for her, most of the time. She was a big woman, always bumbling and looked like someone who would, most probably, get a heart attack, if anyone so much as yelled at her.

Mrs Krishnan heard the commotion. Seeing Arvind, she excused herself from the group of other councilmen and walked over to ask after Tony.

"Hello Eleena, Arvind, Leslie, how are you? Mind if I join you?"

Arvind pulled a chair for her. Seated, they indulged in some small talk. She knew Tony and Arvind were close and he might be upset about his suspension. Carefully, she asked "How is Tony doing?"

"He is well, ma'am," Arvind replied and Leslie added, "He is in Chennai, ma'am."

"Chennai? Why Arvind?"

"Ma'am he is visiting a friend there."

"To investigate a case," Leslie finished his sentence.

"He is suspended, Arvind. What case is he investigating?"

"That's not what he is doing, ma'am. He is just there to meet a friend from academy days."

"Arvind, I know I played a part in his suspension, but I did it for his own good. Trust me, I know how he must be feeling as a father; I would feel the same and I don't blame him. I don't want any harm to come to him and he is in the state of mind right now where he can be dangerous for himself. Please Arvind, I will not ask you again, but if you think I am not against Tony, and that I have his best interest at heart, tell me what he is doing."

Arvind shared a look with Eleena, they both knew that Mrs Krishnan was a good woman. Arvind had felt almost betrayed by Mrs Krishnan's decision, but he didn't blame her for it. In her place, he realized, he would have done the same.

"Ma'am, he is not investigating really, but he is looking into some old case in Chennai. And I know he is suspended, and I don't blame you for it. But you don't know what happened after that. He had lost all hope to live! He was wasting away, as if waiting for death to come."

Mrs Krishnan looked sad and guilty. "I am sorry, Arvind."

"Don't be, ma'am. I would have done the same," Arvind said matter-of-factly.

"I am happy to hear that. You are a good friend, Arvind. And I am glad that you are not holding it against me."

"Not at all, ma'am."

The waiter came over to tell Arvind that his table was ready.

"But Arvind, don't you think this is a short term solution only?" the little voice came from the most surprising source.

"What do you mean, Leslie?"

"I mean, Tony will research some random cases and then what?"

They all looked puzzled now. Shy of the attention, haltingly she said, "Sir, this is a temporary solution, I think. What's the long term solution here, so that he doesn't fall back into depression?"

"Arvind, she may have a point." Eleena said.

"I don't know. I did what I could think of at that moment."

"You are right Leslie, but when I saw Tony last, he was behaving like a man possessed. This might be a short-term solution, but it has worked. And maybe this will help Tony recover fully," Mrs Krishnan said thoughtfully

"It won't, ma'am. You see, I knew someone who had depression, and in such a situation, it is important to look for long term solutions. I mean, sir was depressed because he couldn't solve Sam's case, and now he is researching other cases, looking for something to keep him occupied. But he can't do this all his life. He will have to stop someday with this meaningless exercise and then what will he be left with?"

"You are quite right, Leslie," Eleena said. "But what could be a long term solution?"

"Change of place," she said shortly.

"Chennai is a change of place."

"No. Change to a different city away from Sam's case."

"Oh! She has a point, Arvind! I know you both looked into every angle of Sam's murder. It's unfortunate that every clue into the murder turned up into nothing. I think chasing random tails here might be more harmful than good," Mrs Krishnan said.

"Yes, Tony sir needs to go to a place far away. Maybe take a transfer to another city," Leslie said timidly.

"Oh yes! Away from Marsti, or Tamil Nadu even! Maybe in Kerala?" Eleena piped in.

"Mumbai?" Leslie piped in.

"Mumbai! I could speak to some people, it could be arranged. Mumbai might just be the change of place that Tony needs," Mrs Krishnan added to Leslie's suggestion.

"Mumbai is fast-paced, and the culture is different, everything will be new. It sounds like the perfect place for a fresh start for Tony. And who knows he might even meet somebody there. Someone to love again," Eleena said, excitedly.

"Thomas had invested in a property in Mumbai sometime back. Tony could stay there."

"Oh... Tony may want his own place," Eleena said.

"Wait! Please. Let's consult him before deciding his life."

"But this is for his good, Arru," Eleena said.

"Eleena, it doesn't matter. We can't decide for a man without his consent. I am sorry but this doesn't seem right to me. He is not an invalid and can make his own decisions," Arvind said a little huffily.

"We will see you later, ma'am. Our table is ready. And I hope you will not feel compelled to stop Tony from researching some old case."

"No Arvind. And thank you for telling me, it means a lot. I am still very fond of Tony."

"I know. See you tomorrow, Leslie."

23rd October
Sunday

Pervez picked up Tony from the bus stop in the morning and brought him straight home. His wife, Zeabunisha, dressed in a salwar kameez, head covered with dupatta, and an open smile, welcomed them at the door. She handed Pervez his purse and sent him to work from the door.

"Sorry Anna, he will meet you at lunch. He has taken a half day. He has a meeting with DCP saab this morning and had he come inside, he would have asked for tea and then he would have started talking, and then he would be late, and then he would have cribbed about being late till dinner," she said with endearment in her tone, and a laugh.

She showed him a clean, spacious room, with freshly made bed, on the ground floor of the double storied house. Showing him the bathroom and asking him if he wanted tea before or after breakfast, she handed him a bulky file. "Pervez told me to give this to you. But please, will you have breakfast with the kids once you have freshened up? They will leave for the school soon and they are eager to meet their uncle Tony."

"Of course. I will be out in five minutes."

Tony was enchanted by Pervez Sheikh's five and seven-year-old daughters. The five-year-old was more talkative and introduced herself forthright; the older daughter was shy at first, but opened up when her mother started telling Tony about the stories of the girls' antics. They insisted on taking an off from school to spend the day with Tony uncle and Zeabunisha agreed without resistance. Pervez had apprised his wife about Sam's murder.

Tony was kept amused till Pervez Sheikh came in the afternoon and his daughters rushed into his arms. Tony, tears held in check till then, broke at the sight that was practiced by him for years with Sam. He excused himself to his room.

That night he spoke to Pervez for some time, and after dinner, retired to his temporary room and finally opened the file he had travelled all this way to read.

Tony read through the night, and the next day; he only emerged for lunch and said he wasn't hungry at dinner, but a dinner plate laden with food enough for two people was brought into his room by Pervez's daughters. At 4.00 a.m., when Tony realized he was ravenous, he ended up eating everything on the plate and wishing there was more.

The next day, he met the girls at breakfast and helped them pack their bags for school. The rush of emotions was almost devastating when the girls kissed Tony before leaving on their school bus. He spent another two days locked in his room. Appearing only for lunch and dinner and avoiding the girls at breakfast. He read the witness accounts and the evidence reports.

The girl's name was Nancy Damascus, born in 1984. Her parents had died in a car accident in 1990, and Garry

Damascus, her paternal uncle, was given her custody when she was only six years old. Ruth Damascus, Garry's wife had left him in 1991, the divorce had been mutual. In 2000, Garry had retired from the force. At the age of sixteen, in 2001, Nancy had joined St Angela's College in Coimbatore and had started staying in the college hostel. In January of 2002, the body of a girl aged four, Sheena Scott, was found in Garry Damascus's house when neighbours complained to the local authorities of a foul stench.

The condition in which the girl was found was as horrific as Sam's. But both the murders had taken place years apart. Almost fifteen years apart. Tony didn't believe in chance happening of things, he didn't believe in coincidences. He had to find out more.

27th October Thursday

Arvind hung up the phone happily. He had called Tony, every morning, like the last four days. He was happy that Tony was occupied with something, even if meaningless.

Leslie suddenly squawked and the stapler on her desk fell on the floor. Why she had chosen this job was beyond Arvind. Everything startled her.

"How is Tony now?"

"He is well. Leslie, why did you choose a career with the force when you could have taken up something else? You are a graduate, aren't you?"

"Yes. Tony is still in Chennai?"

"Yes." Arvind replied starting to read the report of car accident on Mall road from the night before.

"What are you and Eleena doing tonight?"

"Huh!?" Arvind looked up surprised. "Nothing, I guess. Why?"

"Thomas is staying out till late tonight and I hate eating alone. And I like Eleena, but I haven't met her much, so...I just wondered, I hoped, that maybe... I wanted to invite you with Eleena, to my house... so..." she said haltingly.

Arvind laughed! He laughed because this plain looking, plain clothed shy woman, sometimes amazed him with her simplicity. He again wondered what had made this sweet natured woman marry a jerk like Thomas.

"I will ask her and if she is free, which I am sure she will be to meet you, we will come over. What time? And shall we bring something?"

Arvind called Eleena at lunch hour and asked her if she would like to go for dinner at Leslie's, expecting that he would have to convince her, but Eleena readily agreed. Apparently, Leslie reminded Eleena of her college friend. Women, their minds and hearts, Arvind surmised, were really a mystery.

Leslie turned out to be a fabulous cook, though she would have ruined her own dinner in the first five minutes if it were not for Arvind's help.

When they reached, Leslie opened the door, wearing jeans and a top, she looked pleasant. Almost pretty. She seated them, on the spacious, luxurious sofa in the living room and went to fetch the tray of juice and almost dropped it when she tripped over her own lush carpet. Arvind held her and stopped the tray from falling over the expensive looking off white carpet and spoiling it.

Arvind was enamoured by Leslie's house. The house, an old property, had been empty for years. Its owners deceased and their kids settled in big cities. It had been just a big broken house for over ten years. But now it looked like a palace. Furnished in light coloured porcelain marble, dark leather sofas, teak and rose wood tables with sparkling glass tops and hand carved chairs with intricate finish, carpets around every sitting area, huge chandeliers, and tall candle lamps, the house looked fit for a king. Leslie must really love her job, he thought, because she definitely didn't need her salary, apart from, maybe, paying the maid in the house.

At the dinner table, Arvind and Eleena decided to serve their host when they saw Leslie trip again while bringing the serving dishes to the dining table.

"So? Thomas told me you were planning on proposing to Eleena. When is the big day?" Leslie asked almost reluctantly, halfway through dinner and Arvind almost choked. He hadn't actually told Thomas Braganza anything like that. He planned to propose to Eleena soon, but he hadn't actually thought of the how or where or even when. Eleena smiled coyly.

"Soon," Arvind mumbled, trying to direct the food in his mouth down the correct pipe.

Eleena led most of the conversations, and asked how Leslie and Thomas had met, how they had fallen in love, or if it was an arranged marriage. She asked whether they had had a wedding and a big reception as well. But got a very short polite reply.

"We met through a colleague of mine.

Didn't date long.

Just a few months.

Got married in the court."

"Didn't you want a big wedding?"

"Thomas didn't want it. His estranged parents live with his brother in Spain. And he doesn't have any family in India. So there was no point in having a big wedding."

"What about your family Leslie?"

"Gone," she replied shortly, and Eleena regretted asking the question immediately.

The rest of the dinner went pleasantly. Leslie, if timorous, turned out to be a gentle, and gracious host.

"When is Tony coming back by the way?" Leslie asked after dinner and a few drinks had helped her loosen up a bit and she wasn't as jumpy as she usually was.

"I don't know. I think he is still investigating that case. He said the case had been very high profile and that's why Pervez sir couldn't send the files on post or email. I know you both think that this is a short term solution, but please don't start again. Let the man do what any father would. I just think we need to trust him and give him time to deal with this as best he can."

Eleena started to argue, but Leslie said she agreed with that.

"Tony does need to do whatever he can, so he doesn't feel like he left any stone unturned."

"Exactly!"

"But I do feel worried about him so far away, in a city where he hardly knows anyone. Here, in Marsti, we were all around to look out for him."

"I know! Arvind, you have to tell him to come back. What if nothing comes out of this line of investigation either? And there is little possibility that this exercise will be fruitful. And he is all alone there. What if he goes under depression again?" Eleena said passionately.

"What can I do?"

"Ask him to do all the research from here."

"He won't come back like that. And I won't ask him to, either."

"If I could take a leave, I would go there myself and convince him to come back," Leslie said sadly.

"Hey! But you can bring him back, Arru. Can't you? And if you were there..." Eleena was saying when Arvind cut her short, "El, he will not listen to me. He is a father who will not rest till the murderer of his child is caught and punished."

"Okay. But we can't let him stay in an unknown city like that! I mean, he knows next to no one in Chennai. We are all here. And once he is back, we could talk him into taking a transfer, like Mrs Krishnan suggested. My maternal aunt stays there with her daughter. She recently got divorced and would be perfect for Tony. I could arrange a chance meeting..."

"Stop! Please! Don't you understand what this man is going through? It will be a wonder if he even gets back to living like he used to before. A few days back I thought I had almost lost my brother. And here you are talking about setting him up like nothing has happened!" he said angrily.

"I am sorry. I didn't mean it like that. I just want Tony to start over again. I love him, too. He's one of the nicest men I know. And moping doesn't help. I know because not too long ago I faced the same. But love helped me recover. It may help him too. That's all I meant. I am sorry Arvind," Eleena said softly, close to tears.

"We should be going now. It's late," Arvind said to Leslie.

Tenderly, taking Eleena's hand, "I know you mean well baby. I am sorry.."

"I am sorry too, Arvind. I didn't mean to be pushy like that."

"I love it when you are pushy, El," he said with a smile.

28th October
Friday

On the 5th day, concerned about Tony hardly stepping out of his room, Pervez asked him to come to the police station for the day. Tony tried to decline, but when Pervez insisted that he wanted Tony to get some fresh air, he relented.

At the police station, Pervez excused himself for a meeting and showed Tony to his own cabin, and left him with Garry's file.

Tony had read and reread the file. The thing that puzzled Tony the most was the similarities in the cases that took place years apart.

On a hunch and with nothing else to keep him occupied, Tony decided to search for cases with the same MO in Chennai. Going year wise, back from 2002, Tony typed in the keywords and started scanning the results. After a few hours, having found nothing, Tony decided to modify his search and 'girl child, molested, raped, beaten, bitten, murdered' were the used key words, together, and then in various combinations.

It was already evening and Pervez had not returned. Tony had a creaking pain in his back and neck from having sat in one position for hours. As he was thinking about going home, he removed the year filter and "Murdered girl in Chennai was beaten and bitten to death" pulled a result that stopped Tony in his thoughts. A girl was found in 2010 after three days of being kidnapped and her body, the article read, had been mutilated to a point that the girl had succumbed to internal bleeding and drugs were found in the child's body too. There were no pictures in the article, but there was a reference of a similar case in 2009. Alert, Tony started searching for cases with similar MO around 2010.

He was still engrossed in reading when Pervez entered in a rush, apologizing for being gone all day.

"It's okay," Tony said without looking up from Pervez's laptop.

"Let's go home. Zeabunisha is waiting for dinner. She's going to kill me when I tell her I had to be gone all day, leaving you alone. What did you have for lunch?"

"Hmmm... yes. Okay."

"What are you doing!?" Pervez asked when Tony still didn't look up. He went around his desk to where Tony was seated at his chair, looking at the laptop.

"Pervez, is it possible to meet the investigating officer of the Garry Damascus case?" Tony asked, finally looking up.

"Why?"

"Is it possible? Can you arrange a meeting?"

"Yes, I suppose so. But why are you interested in this case, Tony? I read the file myself and the guy is in jail. How is this case related to Sam's murder?"

"I have a feeling that not only Sam's case, but a few more could be related to this man. It seems the murder he was found guilty of and punished for, was the first in a series of others that followed."

"What? You mean there are other murders with the same print!?"

"Yes."

"No! That's impossible. Someone would have caught on if that was the case. You are imagining things now, Tony!"

"Anna, no one saw the connection, and maybe that's the reason that a killer is still at large. And, I can't be sure, but it also might be the same killer."

"Garry Damascus was caught with the body in his house. He was sentenced to jail on the statement of his own niece. What you are suggesting is impossible! That murder happened in 2002, Sam was kidnapped in 2016. And all rapists are brutal. All rapists hurt the victim physically, Tony. That's why it's called rape."

"Do all rapists also drug their victims? Do all rapists make sure that not a drop of body fluid is left on the victim? If these murders are related, then we are dealing with a man who is most precise and most dangerous!"

"Garry drugged the girl before raping her?"

"No. that's the only case where the girl was not drugged, but Sam was, and look at this, I found these three cases, right here in Chennai! They were drugged. I need their files too, Pervez."

"Three more cases in Chennai? Why has no one else seen the pattern before!"

"This is not the time to wonder about the 'whys and why nots'. I need your help, Pervez. Will you arrange a meeting with this officer? His name is Ram Gowda; he retired five years back. And I need the case files of these three cases." Tony leafed through the papers he had been making notes on and handed a piece of paper to Pervez who took it looking baffled.

Pervez made a few calls and walked out to his ASI's desk to ask him to find out the case number and police station in-charge for the three cases that Tony wanted to read.

He came back after a few minutes with Ram Gowda's mobile number.

"The case files will take time to dig out, but you can speak to Gowda. If he refuses to meet, then I will find someone to speak and convince him to see you."

Tony made the call and the retired officer sounded drunk as he slurred, but agreed to meet him the next day at Jagruti Bar.

29th October
Saturday

"Why are you interested in this case, Mr George?" Ram Gowda asked when the waiter left, leaving two double Royal Stags for Ram Gowda and a single Teacher's for Tony. The question was asked off-handedly, but was far from causal inquiry.

Tony had told him as soon as they met that he wanted to talk about the Garry Damascus case. He had expected that Ram would not remember which case it was, but the drunk, bearded man just appraised Tony with sharp, although red-rimmed and sloppy eyes. He had sipped on his double whiskey staring at Tony and Tony had returned the stare. When he ordered two more whiskeys for himself, Tony acquiesced to it being a long evening, and ordered himself one too. "This murder maybe connected to my daughter's," Tony said simply.

Ram didn't react. The old officer nodded his head, took another sip of his whiskey and removed a pack of 555 from his pocket. Without saying a word, he got up from his chair, taking his glass, he headed for the door, lighting it before he was out of the door. The manager at the gate saluted Ram.

The air outside the dingy bar was better. Wearing thick glasses, receding hairline, poke-marked face, the officer was muscled, in his early sixties. Pervez had told Tony that Ram Gowda had a clean career record, was divorced and the only negative anyone had said about him was that he drank heavily, though never on duty.

"What do you want to know?"

"Everything," Tony said. Ram Gowda threw his cigarette and stepped on the half-smoked stick.

"Come inside. We need to speak more privately."

Inside the bar, Ram spoke to the manager standing at the door.

The manager led them through the kitchen. A metal staircase led to a small office with low ceiling, a large table, an old computer, a telephone, and a few chairs. The manager left to return with their drinks, a bottle of water and an ashtray. Switching on the AC, he left them alone, closing the door behind him.

"Tell me about your daughter." Ram Gowda asked, and Tony did.

"She was murdered the same way Sheena Scott was," Tony said and Ram looked mildly surprised.

"You have managed to read Garry/Sheena murder files. Haven't you? Don't you know that Garry is in a mental asylum since 2004?"

"No, this I didn't know," Tony was surprised.

"If Sheena's murderer is locked up, then how could this case have anything to do with your daughter?" Ram asked and downed his glass.

Tony took a sip of his own whiskey and told Ram Gowda for the next hour about Sam's murder.

He heard with dawning horror what he himself had suspected during the Garry/Sheena murder investigation. Back then, he had told himself that it was only a false gut feel and nothing more.

Ram Gowda stood quietly, collecting his own thoughts, reliving the days of investigation and then the murder trial. When he finally spoke, his voice sounded weak to his own ears and he cleared his throat.

"Garry Damascus was half crazy when we found him. The child had been murdered for over a week, her body was stinking up his house. I don't think he even realized that the child was in his house. By the end of the trail, he was raving mad. He was sent to a psychiatric facility soon after."

"I am sure that there is a connection between these murders and there have been similar kidnappings and rapes after that also."

Tony had printed out the news reports of the other three murders and showed the file with articles to Gowda. Ram Gowda looked at the file, astonished, unbelieving. Tony was about to say more to present his case when Ram Gowda spoke.

"I always suspected that Garry may not be the murderer."

"What? Why?" Tony asked flabbergasted.

"Because the way the kidnapping was done, the brutality of the crime didn't sit well with the profile of the man we found. We believed and the court agreed that he may have lost his mind after the murder, but the act itself was too cold blooded for a man on the edge of losing his mind. It was an act of a mad man. But a mad man who knows exactly what he is doing. And then, for him to leave the body in his own house like that and be caught was something that I wondered about for a long time," Ram Gowda said.

"Garry Damascus was an officer himself. And not a bad one either. It was clear after speaking to his niece that he was a pedophile, but a murderer? After kidnapping this child and bringing her all the way from Coimbatore to Chennai without being seen, murdering her, but then just leaving her in a cupboard! It didn't add up."

"Did he confess to the murder?"

Ram took a pause contemplating and replied, "Yes and no."

"What?"

"I told you, he was half mad when we caught him. Actually, I can't even say we caught him because when we raided his house, he was just sitting on a chair, next to an open window, maybe to get away from the stink. He didn't open the door when we rang the bell, when we knocked. He didn't move when we broke the door down. He didn't say anything when we tried to talk to him. He didn't even react when we brought the body out into the living room. It was crawling with maggots, Mr George. And Garry simply scrunched his nose at the offensive smell. And then he looked at the body finally and started to laugh. It was the most hysterical laugh I have ever heard. That was the first time I thought that maybe someone else had murdered the child and kept her there to frame Garry Damascus."

"Why would anyone do that?"

"Exactly! And during our investigation, we didn't find anyone with the motive to either."

"What else made you think he could be framed?"

"What?" asked Ram Gowda, looking distant, as if reliving that day.

"Oh! The second time I thought he couldn't have done it was when we investigated the drugs found in his house. We caught hold of all the local drug suppliers and no one had sold any to this man. Mr George, this man was pumped full of drugs when we found him. He had been taking drugs for some time, his blood reports said. We found drugs in his house, Ecstasy and Cocaine. But none of the local drug suppliers recognized him. And according to his colleagues, Garry was a social drinker but had never been known to take drugs."

"Was that all?"

"No, the last part was most baffling, to me. Why, Mr George, would a man travel to Coimbatore from Chennai to kidnap a child? Garry Damascus hadn't known Sheena Scott or her family. The kidnapping was done so smoothly, but if he had to just randomly kidnap a child, why would he take the trouble of going to and bringing back the child from over 500 kms away?"

"Maybe he had gone for some work and found the child?"

"Found the child? We are talking about a kidnapping. How do you transport a child?"

"Car?"

"Yes, but his car was an old Fiat that had a flat tire when we found it. It looked like it hadn't been washed in months and had cobwebs inside too! It didn't look like it had been serviced in years. I doubt that car had travelled to Coimbatore and back."

"But can you rule it out?"

"No. And that is why Garry was given a life sentence. Everything pointed towards him being the murderer, but my gut kept telling me there was something wrong with the narrative. That's it, you see."

Tony sat quietly. He had come to meet Ram Gowda for answers, but the officer himself had questions.

"You too have read the files, Mr George. Do you think the case is as simple as it seems?"

"I don't know, sir. But I know that there is someone out there who is killing the same way that Garry was jailed for. And I don't believe it is a coincidence," Tony replied after a moment's thought.

Tony spoke to Ram Gowda till 2 a.m. He had called Pervez around 11.00 p.m. to tell him that he would be staying at the hotel as he had had to drink and would be late.

"*Thambi,* this is your own house and you can bring the bottle home if you want. Just come home and call me on my mobile once you reach because the doorbell will wake up Zeabunisha. I will open the door. And don't argue with me right now," Pervez had said caringly.

"Is it possible to meet Garry Damascus?" Tony asked as he waited for the cab.

Some kids were lighting crackers on the road, dancing around the fire in celebration. Sam had followed this ceremonial ritual too, with much enthusiasm. Tony shut his eyes tight to black out the memories.

"I will check and call you tomorrow," Ram Gowda slurred.

30th October
Sunday

Garry Damascus looked old and frail, sitting in a chair next to a barred window, with his hands on the railing and nails scratching at the faded paint.

Garry was wearing a stained white shirt and pyjamas with the hospital name embossed on the chest. An aluminum jug of water and steel glass stood on the table, both chained to the wall. His empty food plate had just been cleared when Tony came in. He didn't notice Tony as he came in and sat on the end of his metal bed.

"Hello," Tony said.

"He will not reply, *Anna*. He rarely speaks," said the attendant from the door, looking at his watch and then towards Tony.

"My name is Anthony George. You are Garry Damascus?" Tony asked and again got no response. Garry continued to stare out of the window.

"Inspector Garry?" Tony tried and this time he was sure a faint smile touched Garry's lips.

"I am here to ask about Sheena Scott." No reaction. No recognition at the name. He didn't even flinch.

"I am an inspector too. I am Senior PI at Marsti town." This fell on empty ears too.

"Is he always like this?" Tony asked the attendant and he nodded yes.

"Has anyone ever come to meet him? Family or friends?"

"No sir. Since I came to work here, no one has come to meet him. They say he is a rapist. He sometimes gets violent and sometimes he starts to throw things. It's one of the long term effects of doing heavy drugs. But he is usually sitting there and not talking and not reacting. *"Avar paittiyukkarattanama!"* he said in a heavily accented dialect, stating the obvious.

"Since when have you been working here?"

"2009 I think," the attendant replied after a quick calculation in his mind.

"He had a wife and a niece. Can you check in your files if Ruth Damascus or Nancy Damascus ever came here to see him?" Tony requested, but the attendant and the guard were looking over Tony's shoulder towards Garry, who had started rubbing his crotch, still looking outside the window, but now he was smiling.

"Does he do this often too?"

"Yes sir, since I have been attending to him, he has done this a couple of times. But when he was brought in, they say he used to, often. He would suddenly get violent or start touching himself or other men and women," he said.

"Garry? Do you remember Ruth? She's your wife. Do you miss her?" Garry didn't pay attention.

"Do you remember Nancy?" and the man suddenly started rubbing himself vigorously. His smile wide, his remaining blackened teeth visible, he started nodding.

Tony tried to control his anger, telling himself that this man was not in his senses.

"Can you tell me anything about Nancy?" Tony asked and Garry stuck his hand down his pyjamas and started chanting something. Tony bent closer to make out what he was saying and heard, "It's not hurting, Nancy, you're loving it. You just don't know it. Touch me, Nancy," he was repeating over and over, his voice lustful, soft, eager, angry and demanding.

Tony got up to hit the man but stopped himself with effort, somehow, and stormed out. At the reception, he asked to see the doctor in charge of Garry.

Ram Gowda had spoken to the doctor and told her that Inspector Anthony George would be visiting to see Garry and might have questions for her. As Tony entered, the doctor, an elderly lady with big eyes and bigger smile with very white teeth, greeted him warmly, asked him for tea or coffee, and without waiting for an answer, dwelled into Garry's medical history, setting aside the papers in her hand immediately.

"Garry Damascus has been diagnosed with substance induced sexual dysfunction, substance-induced persisting dementia, hallucinogen-persisting perception disorder, and sleep disorder that is manifesting itself into a kind of personality disorder lately. His condition has only deteriorated since he has been admitted. We even tried shock treatments, but nothing so far has worked."

"Doctor, has anyone come to see Garry at the hospital?"

"Not that I know of. Why do you ask?"

"He reacted very strongly when I said his niece's name. He started to get sexually aroused, but you just said he has sexual dysfunction?"

The doctor called the reception, "Have someone tie patient no. 108's hands to the bed. He is getting another episode," she said into the phone and turned back to Tony.

"Garry Damascus does react very strongly to that name. His case files say that he was charged with raping this girl when she was eight years old. We have had incidents where he has tried to touch male and female doctors and nurses inappropriately, but the name he takes is always Nancy. Some of the things he says during these episodes of lunacy are shameful and I have wanted to strike him hard, many a times myself. But I am a doctor and this is a mad man. His sexual dysfunction means that he does not get an erection, but he rubs himself hard enough to make himself bleed, and that is why he has to be tied at such times."

31st October
Monday

Ruth Damascus had remarried and was now Ruth Sequiera. Tony found her home alone as her husband had taken the kids out for Deepavali shopping. Tony had called in advance to ask her if she could talk to them and she had agreed, unhappily.

She enquired, worried, if Nancy was in any trouble and was relieved when Tony told her that he was only looking at the case files and wanted to talk to her and Nancy. He told her that no one was in trouble and this was not official either, so she could choose to not divulge any information.

She didn't have much to share, apart from how she had suspected her husband to be a pedophile when she had found questionable pictures of children in his cupboard. Her suspicions, Ruth said, had disappeared when she saw how loving and caring Garry was with Nancy, but he had wanted a divorce by then.

"I was shocked when I heard about what Garry had done to Nancy. She was a beautiful, angelic child. If I had had any idea, I would have done something to help her. To save her." She broke down.

She told Tony that she had tried to contact and talk to Nancy when she found out everything, but Nancy had refused saying she didn't need anyone anymore. Nancy had accused her aunt of knowingly abandoning her when she should have taken Nancy with her.

Ruth said she felt somewhat responsible for what had happened and wished she hadn't left Nancy and should have kept in touch with her even after the divorce. "I never suspected anything like this and I had tried to meet Nancy after the divorce, but Garry warned me to stay away from her."

"I have no blood relation with her, so I had no way to legally demand meeting her. But I have since regretted not trying. She was so shy sometimes. I have wondered if maybe she was so because of what Garry was doing to her. I have wondered if her shyness was a disguise for fear that I misread," she said sniffling.

"Do you know where Nancy is now? I want to talk to her."

"I don't know anything apart from the fact that she was in college in Coimbatore. Maybe you could find the details from there," she said and requested Tony to inform her when he found her. "I want to apologize to her again. I hope she will forgive me now."

Tony called the college, but remembered it was a Sunday when the phone went unanswered. He called the hostel number from Google and the warden, after some convincing, told him that Nancy had been a good, well-behaved, quiet girl who didn't have any friends and didn't go out other than for her jogs. She told Tony that maybe her teachers, some of whom were still teaching, could tell him more, but he would have to call the principal to speak to them the next day.

"Nancy did have a room-mate, Asha Pillai. She was maybe her only friend. You could speak to her," the warden said and gave her last known number.

Tony called Asha Pillai, assistant manager at a national bank in Coimbatore. She told Tony she couldn't speak before evening as she was busy with guests, and asked him to call after 7.00 p.m.

When she spoke to Tony, she said the same thing that the warden and her aunt Ruth had said.

Asha said she had tried to ask Nancy a few times about her childhood and Nancy had broken down crying and refused to talk. She also told Tony that she had had nightmares, where she spoke softly sometimes and woke up yelling a few times.

"But the dreams got worse after a date she went out on and then she had moved out of the room." Tony asked what she said in her nightmares and Asha told him that after the initial few months, she had stopped paying attention, but mostly she moaned and said things like 'no, it hurts, please stop' and sometimes she had cried out for her mom and dad, saying '*appa, amma,* pls come'. Mostly she just cried, sometimes loudly, as if in pain and sometimes softly as if she was sad."

"How did the nightmares get worse after her date?"

"Her nightmares got more violent. She would shout and thrash and yell and mumble loudly. Not just me, but even girls in rooms close to ours were troubled by it, but everyone felt bad for Nancy. She was so awkward and lonely, no one said anything to her. But then I couldn't take it and I asked her if she could request the warden for a separate room and she agreed immediately."

"Do you know who she went on this date with?"

"Yes, his name was Murli Iyenger. He was my husband's friend, and in senior college, we were in the same circle. After college, he took up a job in Canada and his family shifted there soon after. I tried asking my husband a few times if Murli had ever spoken about what happened on the date with Nancy, but apparently Murli never spoke about it."

"Do you know anyone who would have his contact number or address in Canada?"

"My husband might have his number. I will SMS you the number, if he does."

Asha Pillai messaged Murli's number ten minutes later.

Tony called Murli Iyenger's number thrice and got no answer. He sent a message asking Murli to call back and that it was in connection to a murder. At 12.30 a.m., Tony got a call back from a very scared Murli. He assured Murli that he was not in any problem and asked about Nancy.

Tony had expected that Murli would not remember her, but the immediate reply came, "Nancy Damascus? From my college? What has she done?" This surprised Tony.

"Why do you think she has done something?"

"Well, you are asking me about her... so I gathered. But, why are you calling me? I haven't seen or spoken to her in years," he said quickly.

"Yes, but you did know her. You in fact dated her. Isn't that right?"

"Wrong! I never dated her!"

"Did you not take her out for a movie once?"

"Yes, but I never spoke to her after that. I have nothing to do with her."

"Relax, Mr Iyenger; I just need to know what happened that day when you took her out."

"Nothing happened. Why are you asking me this after so many years?"

Tony was losing his cool but his voice was calm, "Mr Iyenger, I have personal reasons for asking this. I am not talking as an inspector. I request you to please tell me what happened that day."

"You mean I am not a part of any investigation?" he asked carefully and Tony knew that this guy was too assured now and hoped he wouldn't lie.

"No. But I would appreciate if you would tell me. Please."

"But if I decide to not tell you anything, I won't be charged for not cooperating with the police?"

"No," Tony said, scared that Murli would not speak now.

There was silence on the line. Tony was about to say thank you and hang up when Murli spoke.

"She broke my finger, officer."

"What!?" Tony asked astonished. He was sure he had heard wrong. "Could you repeat that, Mr Iyenger?"

"I said she broke my finger. Like actually broke it and it had to be plastered back."

Carefully, Tony asked, "Why did she break your finger Mr Iyenger?"

"I don't know. Because she was crazy, maybe."

"How did she break your finger? Did she hit you with something??"

"No, she did it with her own hands. I think she twisted it. But I am not sure. It was so painful that I kind of blacked out. Is she in trouble officer?"

"No," replied Tony and got a disappointed 'oh' with a sigh.

"But she could be if you could just explain a little better why did she break your finger? Where? And How?"

"But I won't be involved in any police case?"

"No. Absolutely not. We are not concerned with you. But it would be best if you tell me everything from start to finish in detail."

"Well, one day I saw her in the library and asked her for a movie and she said yes. In the theatre, this girl was sitting right next to me, shoulder to shoulder, and she was crossing her legs and then uncrossing, so to calm her down, I put my hand on her lap. And then she turned to me and started moaning. She liked it, so I started to massage her thighs more, and she started moaning more. And then she turned to me, so I kissed her. And then she took my hand that was caressing her thigh in her own hands, and she broke my finger!"

"Do you think she was maybe resisting and not moaning in pleasure, Mr Iyenger?"

"What? Of course not! She came to the movie with me of her own free will. I didn't force her. And I know the difference between a moan and resistance. She licked my finger before breaking it! She was just shy maybe," he said, trying to justify the act and pass it off as nothing.

"Did you say she licked your finger before breaking it?"

"Yes. See! That's why I said she's crazy," he said exasperated. "She just picked my hand, licked the index finger and broke it with her own hands. And then she said, 'If you tell anyone, I will kill you'."

1st November
Tuesday

Tony called Nancy's college principal in the morning and the principal agreed, after much explaining, to let Tony speak to two of Nancy's teachers who still taught at the college. Tony took the afternoon flight to Coimbatore, carrying nothing but Nancy Damascus's file in a plastic bag and his wallet.

At the airport, in Coimbatore, Tony searched for St Angela's College on Google and was surprised that Ram Gowda had overlooked the fact that Sheena Scott had been kidnapped from a park in the same area. He booked a cab and checked the case file. He checked again and saw that the distance of the park was less than seven kms from Nancy's college. He wondered if Garry had come to meet Nancy, and if that was the case, then Sheena's kidnapping might not have been planned.

Tony spoke to Nancy's teachers at the college, but none had anything to say that was new. Tony asked if they had noticed any form of aggression in Nancy's behaviour or heard of any incident involving her and they said she was an above average student, but there were never any complaints about her.

Before leaving, Tony met the principal to see if Nancy's records had any other address for her or where she took admission after St Angela's. The principal refused to disclose any information, and Tony had to tell him that he was looking into Nancy's case because it might be connected to other rapes and murders since. The principal reluctantly told Tony that he had helped Nancy by trying to counsel her when the case had come out.

"I tried my best to talk her into seeking professional help, but she refused."

"What made you think that she needed counselling, sir?"

"The kids here call me father out of respect for my garb, but I try to be one in a pragmatic sense, too. Nancy was an introvert child, but after the case came out, kids started talking about it. Naturally. And I found that Nancy went further into her shell. Her warden had complained a few times that Nancy would shout at night, and I asked her not to say anything to Nancy. If the child was going through some pain, I wanted to heal her suffering, not aggravate it. I had a talk with Nancy after the police had called her for questioning. They had to take the school's permission, but no one was allowed to speak to her, till after her statement was recorded. While talking to her, I realized that the trauma of her childhood, and the case were both taking a toll on her mental health. Rape scars a person for life, Anthony, and the wounds, I have seen, never heal fully. But when she refused, I didn't want to pressurize her," he said melancholically.

"When her uncle was finally sentenced, she came to me and requested that she wanted to leave the college and the city. When I asked her where she planned to go from here, she didn't have an answer. So I suggested that she take admission in a college in Bangalore where my friend is the trustee and

I know the principal too. I told Nancy that she would be safe there. Thankfully, she agreed."

"Sir, did you find any violent streak in Nancy's behaviour?" Tony asked and saw the surprise and anger dawn in the principal's eyes.

"No! What a thing to ask! Nancy was one of the most mild-mannered and sweet children to have studied here. Even after all that she suffered, I never saw a hint of anger in her, not even for that godforsaken man that was her own blood, her uncle. Never did I ever hear the child speak above a whisper, Anthony! Why would you ask that? I wanted her to get counselling for her emotional pain, not for any other reason. In fact, when she finally got into this college in Bangalore, she was really happy. It was possibly the only time I saw her smile openly," he finished, fondly.

"Sir, did you know that the child who was murdered by Nancy's uncle was kidnapped from a park close to this college?"

"Yes, of course, I had read about it in the newspapers. It's really sad what happened with that child too. Some men, like this monster Garry, deserve the worst punishment in hell," he said passionately.

Tony thanked the old man and decided to meet Sheena Scott's family. He took a cab to the building listed as their address, but the watchman at the gate told Tony that no one by that name lived in that flat anymore. At Tony's behest, the watchman allowed him to meet the building secretary.

The building secretary came to the gate and Tony told him that he wanted to meet the Scott family for a murder investigation. The building secretary said the Scotts had sold their flat almost a decade ago. They had not left any forwarding address, and he had no knowledge of where they went or if they were even in Coimbatore anymore.

Tony knew that he may need to take Pervez's help in locating the Scotts, but decided that it could wait. He was eager to know what happened to Nancy. He wanted to see for himself that the child who had endured so much had finally lived happily. He wanted to see this brave girl who had made herself strong enough to have not just the mettle but the courage to break the bones of the boy who had tried again to touch her without her consent. Tony wanted to know that some girls overcame their monsters and didn't get buried like his own daughter.

He called the mobile number of the principal of Galore College of Commerce, Bangalore, but she refused to disclose any information and said it was unethical to be dragging a disturbed child in an investigation that had nothing to do with her. When Tony told her his own daughter was raped and killed and he was investigating this case to see if there was any connection between the two, the principal, politely told him that she was sorry to hear it, and then sternly continued that he would have to go through the procedure and get a warrant if he needed any information about Nancy.

Tony booked the 9.00 p.m. flight for Bangalore and brought a can of deodorant from a shop on the way.

Tony called Sushila Rao, the principal of Galore College, again from the airport, and tried to reason with her, but she still refused.

"And if you want my appointment, call the school clerk and he will set it up. As it is, I can't take any appointments for a few weeks. Deepavali vacation is going on right now, and the college building is under repairs and renovations. The school will reopen on 5th November and with the work going on, it's going to be impossible to meet you. Call him after 15th November and we will speak then," she said.

Tony spent the night at the airport – awake, eager, waiting for the morning.

2nd November
Wednesday

He called Mrs Sushila Rao at 8.00 a.m. sharp. Her refusal didn't deter Tony. "Ma'am will you be at home today?" Tony had asked desperately and the principal curtly replied, "No. I will be at the college. I told you I am very busy till the 15th, Inspector.

He took a cab from the airport to Galore College.

He couldn't wait till 15th November. It was almost two months since his daughter was taken from him. And if there was even the faintest chance that Nancy could lead him to the murderer, if not Sam's then the other girls who had been killed in Chennai, he was going to meet her. His personal feelings aside, Tony felt in his guts that there was more to the Garry Damascus case than what met the eye.

A peon sat droning at the gate and didn't bat an eyelid when Tony woke him up and asked the directions to the principal's office. The uniformed man, legs spread out, eyes half closed, simply pointed in the direction and said first floor.

The clerk sitting outside Principal Sushila's office was more alert and refused to allow him entry and only called the principal when Tony refused to budge until he met her.

"Principal ma'am is busy right now. She can't meet you," he said curtly when he had finished the short call to the principal.

"I will wait till she is free," Tony said adamantly and took a seat on the bench chair in the waiting area.

Tony had to wait three hours before the principal called him inside.

Dressed in a white and gold Kanjivaram saree, wearing a gold mangalsutra, heavy gold earrings, and gold rimmed spectacles, the fair, plump lady sat at the desk staring at Tony, like he was something unpleasant under her nose.

"Inspector Anthony, I have half a mind to call the Asst. Commissioner, who was a classmate of my husband, and make a complaint against your rowdy behaviour. I will not do so because you told me about the tragedy that has befallen your daughter. But let me tell you in clear words, I do not approve of this behaviour and nor am I willing to reveal any information unless your questioning is part of an official investigation," said the woman judiciously.

"It is lunch hour now. I need to have my medication after eating. I request you to kindly leave and come back only when you have an appointment,," she finished briefly.

"Ma'am, hear me out please. I have reasons to believe that there is a serial killer out there, who might or might not be connected to my daughter's murder, but I am sure, is connected to the murders of at least three other little girls," Tony pleaded, knowing the official investigation, if handed to Tony at all, would not be started immediately.

"Three other murders? Then why is this not an official investigation? Inspector Anthony, my husband is a senior lawyer and I know what an official police investigation procedure is. I will need to be convinced beyond doubt that Nancy's information is vital to your personal inquiry."

Tony told her about the similarities between the three other cases in Chennai and Sheena's murder, and how they were similar to even Sam's murder.

"But this is all circumstantial evidence, and these cases have been closed for years now. To reopen, not one but these three Chennai murders, with Sheena's, for which a man has already been convicted, will take time and I don't have the time, ma'am. I need to be sure before I go to my senior authorities. A suspended officer's word, suspicions, and some half-baked theories will amount to nothing otherwise."

"Anthony, what you are saying is not only appalling, but also most dreadful and worrying," she said. "I can understand why meeting Nancy is so important for you, but I don't know where she is, my son. First thing for you to know is that I, with the help of my husband, had helped Nancy change her name to Emma John. She had taken her father's first name. Though not many people in Bangalore knew about Nancy's identity, there were rumours and that had disturbed her. I felt most empathetic about what the child had been through. Can you imagine a child being sexually abused for years? I suppose you can understand," she said when she saw Tony's face. "Anyway, the only time she called me after leaving college was to tell me that she was getting married in Tiruchirappalli. That's it. She didn't invite us. I and my husband would have definitely attended her wedding otherwise. She just said she was getting married and wanted to thank me and my husband for our help. She never made any friends here, that much I know because I kept a keen eye on her, from afar, to make sure no one bothered her. She was so vulnerable. I am childless, Inspector. I offered Emma to come live with us, as our daughter. But she refused."

"Ma'am, did she tell you who she was marrying or where in Tiruchirappalli she was staying?"

"No. I wish I had won enough of her trust and affection, but I don't hold it against her. I just hope she is happy, wherever she is."

They spoke for another hour; Tony noting down everything that he felt was important. He had been making notes of every interview and about everything.

He called Pervez Sheikh from a hotel near Bangalore airport. His flight at 07.30 a.m. in the morning had a stopover in Chennai and he would be in Tiruchirappalli by 11.00 a.m., he told Pervez.

"Pervez, I will need a contact in Tiruchirappalli. Someone who can dig up some information, maybe an officer."

"Tony, I hope this is not a wild goose chase. But if you are onto something, then you might break a big case. I have the files you wanted on those three murders. I can't email these files to you either, but you can pick them up when you are back."

Tony didn't know if meeting Nancy/ Emma was more important than reading the other files, but his gut feeling told him the next stop had to be Tiruchirappalli.

Pervez Sheikh called back a few hours later with the contact number of Sub Inspector Dashrath Kumaran.

3rd November
Thursday

Tony called PSI Dashrath Kumara after checking into a hotel near the airport and gave his hotel name and address. He had to decide if he was going to contact the commissioner before investigating the other cases or as soon as he had met with Nancy. He felt sure that once he found Nancy, the case would make more sense.

Sometime in the afternoon, while Tony was napping, the doorbell rang. Tired but immediately awake, Tony opened the door to find himself looking down at a short, thin man with silky, long, dark hair and dark complexion, wearing a pink Nike T-shirt and loose jeans. The man said a loud 'hello' and entered Tony's room, slipping under his arm.

"So you are Inspector Anthony," the man said rather than asked, appraising Tony.

"What can I do, sir?" he asked in a falsetto, heavily accented voice, seating himself on a plastic chair that stood next to a low plastic table.

"I need to find a girl. Can you help?"

"I can find you as many girls as you want, *Anna*. But everything has a price," he said but at the look of anger on Tony's face, his grin disappeared.

"Which girl and why?"

"Her name was Nancy Damascus. She changed it to Emma John in 2003. She got married here in the year 2012, and she might have taken her husband's last name thereafter."

In shock and surprise, Dashrath Kumaran looked at Tony.

"Sir, you are not joking. Are you?"

"No," Tony said simply, and sat down on the bed.

"Sir, this is a big city. Not as big as Chennai, but it is big. And to find a girl whose last name also you don't know, sir, is not going to be easy. Plus, this can't be done legally, sir."

"I know. But I am told you can get this done. Now, can you? Just yes or no."

"Of course I can! And Pervez sir is my idol. He has told me to help you in any way possible, and so I will. But this is highly dangerous. If somebody finds out, I will lose my job. So I will have to... you know, sir.. and it won't be cheap either. And there is no guarantee, mind you."

"I understand. How much?"

"I will be able to tell you that, but not now. Do you know anything else about this girl?"

"Her birthday is 9th January 1984, she would be thirty-three years old now. I think her husband is from Tiruchirappalli, but I don't know for sure." Tony didn't trust this man who wore a police uniform, and indulged in illegal activities. He decided against telling Dashrath more about Nancy's past.

"Okay. I will call you once I figure out how to do this. But remember sir, this will be an expensive affair," Dashrath said and looked satisfied when Tony nodded.

5th November
Saturday

The inspector called Tony to tell him that he had found a court receiver who was ready to help dig up Emma John's marriage certificate.

"Meet him at 5.30 at the civil court and he will do the needful. Anthony sir, this man is going to cost you 50,000 rupees, 10,000 advance, which he will keep whether he can find the file or not, and the rest you will have to pay him once the work is done."

"Dashrath, isn't 50,000 a little steep for just a name?" Tony asked.

"He says he's a poor man and has a daughter of marriageable age, and record room job doesn't bring many opportunities for these people to make money off the books."

Tony didn't say anything else and Dashrath sent him the man's phone number.

7th November
Monday

Tony guessed Hari, the court receiver's age to be around thirty-five years. Too young to have a girl of 'marriageable age'. Tony smiled, but didn't say anything. Tony gave him the envelope of 10,000 rupees once they were in a small records room.

"Do you have the name?" Tony asked.

"Sir, this is the record room of property cases. I will have to pay the clerk for the keys to that room which I will do tomorrow, and tomorrow I will start searching at 6.00 p.m. It has all been set up. You can come by 7.00 p.m. By then, there is no one at the court.

Tony went back to his hotel to find Dashrath Kumaran waiting at the reception. Without a word, he followed Tony to his room. Once inside, the door closed behind them, before Tony could ask anything, Dashrath spoke.

"This Nancy Damascus was the girl who was raped by her uncle. Why are you searching for her, Inspector Anthony?" he asked, hostile.

"Why are you concerned about it, Dashrath? If you want money too, I can pay it."

"No, this is about right and wrong. I have a ten-year-old boy but I always wanted a daughter. This girl has been through the worst at such a young age. I have to know that she is not in any problem. And if you are searching for her to make any problem, I will not have any part in it and I will not allow it."

Tony looked at Dashrath, realizing that he had misjudged the man. Corrupt, he may be, but his heart was in the right place.

Tony told Dashrath what he had found till then, and Dashrath listened somberly.

"Sir, a couple of years back, there was a kidnapping of a child from my area and her body was found after over twenty days, decomposed. But the doctors had been certain that she was raped," Dashrath told Tony.

"It might be connected, but till now, the only similarities between the cases have been the MO, the modus operandi."

"This child's body was found in a gunny bag in a pond; she had died of internal bleeding. But other than that, the doctors hadn't been able to make out much. We never found any other clue in the case. The child belonged to a slum nearby and the parents hadn't even realized she was missing till late that night. I want to check the files again. And maybe I can be of more help than that."

"How?"

"Sir, I can find out if there were other such cases here. If there have been, then indeed Nancy Damascus may be the link."

"How much do you need for it?"

"Nothing sir!" he said offended. "I told you, I always wanted a daughter. A little angel. I will do this for the child I never had. For your daughter. For Nancy Damascus. For Sheena Scott, and for all others," he said emotionally.

"Give me a couple of days, sir. And you don't have to pay any more money to the court receiver. The rest of the 40,000 rupees was for me. I will speak to him myself and I will find Nancy alias Emma John."

8th November
Tuesday

Tony went to the court and searched for the file with the court receiver Hari till eleven that night, but didn't find it. Hari promised to call Tony as soon as he had the register and told him that they would have to leave for the day as he had to be back at the court the next day.

10th November
Thursday

Dashrath came to Tony's hotel room in the afternoon, laden with files.

"Sir, in all, there are two more cases with the same MO and one other girl who was never found, but her age is a match. I have also brought the case file of the girl who was kidnapped from my area. Sir, this does look like a serial killer. I am surprised that no one saw the similarities before."

Tony quietly took the files and started going through the cases, making certain notes and taking down dates.

"Dashrath, did you find any cases other than these?"

"No sir, but a lot of crimes go unregistered. In all, there are thirty-eight police stations with eighteen zonal divisions here. If there are other cases, then I will need more time to find the files sir. These are what I got from talking to the constables at the police stations and they told me only from their memory. Finding out all the files by the same method will take days, maybe even a month, and we will need to make the investigation official if we are to proceed in that direction."

"Look at these dates. Sheena Scott was kidnapped from Coimbatore in January 2002, when Nancy was studying there. Nancy was in Bangalore from 2003 till 2006. The three cases that I found in Chennai were reported on February 2008, November 2009, and July 2010. These are the Tiruchirappalli cases and the abductions were reported dated July 2012, august 2013, and January 2015 is when the case was filed in your police station, and then September 2015. And we know Nancy was in Tiruchipalli from 2012."

"What are you saying, sir? Is this the link between the murders?"

"This is the link to the killer! And this is the link between Nancy Damascus, and the murderer." Tony said, frantically. He started pacing the small room.

"I don't understand sir." Dashrath was looking dumbfounded at the paper in front of his eyes, unable to comprehend what Tony was saying.

"Nancy was in Coimbatore when Sheena Scott was kidnapped, and she has been in Tiruchirappalli since 2011/ 2012, I would guess. I need to find this girl, Dashrath. If she was in Chennai during these other murders, then we have our link!"

Tony told Dashrath to find out where the court receiver was on finding Nancy's file. "This is a serial killer Dashrath! And he may be the one who took my Sam too! I am so close to him! I can feel it! Call that guy and find me Nancy Damascus, Dashrath!"

"Sir, shouldn't we go to the authorities now? We have enough evidence to have all these files reopened and then we can investigate better. The law machinery will be on our side."

"No! This man is very clever; he has evaded the police for so long. What if he disappears? We don't know who he is and we don't have any other clue to find him. Nancy is our only clue and he could kill Nancy. I will never find this bastard! I have to kill him, Dashrath. I have to find him and kill him myself!" Tony was raving like a man possessed.

"How will the killer find out about a police investigation, sir?" he asked soberly.

"How will you keep the news of a serial killer in Tamil Nadu out of the newspapers?" Tony shouted, walking even faster.

Dashrath knew what Tony meant and dialled the court receiver's number from his phone.

"Sir, Hari says he will have the file by tonight. There had been a pest control at the court a few months back and some of the files were mixed. If Nancy got married in Tiruchirappalli and has registered with the court, then we will have the file tonight, sir. Please calm down, sir." Dashrath pleaded and offered his opened, half drunk, warm bottle of beer to Tony. Tony sat down, took the bottle, and said cheers with the most dangerous and treacherous smile Dashrath had seen.

Dashrath and Tony drank beer and worked on the files till 1.00 a.m. Dashrath went to sleep on the chair in Tony's room and was awakened at 2.00 a.m. by his phone ring which he picked up without seeing.

"Sir, wake up!" he said with a start, shaking Tony awake. "Sir, he found the marriage register!"

Dashrath spoke into the phone and nodded, telling Tony that tomorrow, before work, the receiver would drop the register's photocopy at Tony's hotel.

"Ask him, what is the name on the file? Is it still Emma John or something else?" Tony asked tersely and Dashrath repeated the same into the phone.

"Sir, it's Leslie Braganza!" Dashrath said, incredulous, flabbergast, and the look was mirrored in Tony's eyes.

"Hari, I will collect the copy from you myself tomorrow. Be careful that no one finds out about this. I will call you," Dashrath spoke automatically and hung up.

"Sir, there must be some mistake. It can't be Leslie!" Dashrath said softly, almost to himself and Tony did a double take.

"How the heck do you know Leslie Braganza?"

"Sir, she was the constable with my police station. She joined us in early 2012, I think. And before that..." Dashrath stopped midsentence and a look of horror slowly replaced that of disbelief.

"Sir, Leslie was posted in Chennai before that! I know because her husband told us at a party once."

"I signed her papers! How did I not see her work history?" Tony asked himself.

Both hurriedly got on their mobile phones. Tony called Pervez to check the work record of Constable Leslie Braganza in Chennai and to check if there were any cases with Sheena's MO in Bangalore. Dashrath called one of his own constables and asked to pull out the file of Leslie Braganza and WhatsApp him each page of the file.

They got off the phone and Tony slumped on the bed. Dashrath crashed on the floor when he dropped heavily into the plastic chair, missing it by an inch.

11th November
Friday

Tony took the 9.05 a.m. flight from Tiruchirappalli and reached Chennai at 10.10. Checking his watch constantly, he rushed out of the airport where Pervez was waiting for him.

"Tony, you should talk to the DCP. He is my friend. Even off the records, he can help you in your investigation. You can't do this alone. You shouldn't do this alone, man! This man is dangerous and you don't even know who he is or where he is from. He could be just about anyone. You could get blindsided, Tony! And in our job that can be a grave mistake, perilous." Pervez said without any greetings.

"I can't involve anyone right now Pervez; you have to trust my decision. This girl has done her best to run away from her past. I don't even know yet how the killer is connected to her. How can I throw this child to the wolves? You know what the DCP will do. This is a big case and he will immediately take custody of Leslie and start with her interrogations. Don't you know how cops question a girl?"

"Tony! This 'child' is as old as you! This child is a married woman and there has been a trail of dead little girls wherever she has gone. No matter what method the police use on her, the killer will be caught! You can't do this alone from here on!"

"I am not alone though. Am I, *Anna?"* Tony asked seriously.

"You know I am with you, one hundred percent, brother. Okay. In the dashboard are the files you asked for. I have contacted my friends in Bangalore and they will find out if there have been any similar cases reported from 2003 to 2006. In Chennai I will check where she was posted and during that period if there were other cases reported. What else do you need?"

"Nothing. Just drop me to the bus station now."

"You are going back straight away? Without meeting Zeabunisha and the kids?"

"I will come and see them as soon as I have this killer, Pervez. But right now, I need to get to Marsti. I need to talk to Leslie in person and this really can't wait. You understand, *Anna*?"

"Yes, I do. Tony, if you want I can take a leave and come with you to Marsti. This situation is far more dangerous than you are giving it credit of being."

"Don't worry. I have someone in Marsti who has always had my back. Arvind Maran, my brother." Tony said confidently.

The bus to Marsti had just left and the next was hours away. Without thinking twice, Tony booked a private cab that was asking for more money than a flight would have charged.

"I will call you as soon as I have the files. And please just call me if you need me," Pervez smiled and hugged Tony.

On the way to Marsti, Tony called Arvind and told him he would be reaching home by 5.00 p.m. and was glad to hear the happiness in Arvind's voice.

Arvind was waiting at Tony's house when he reached and jumped up to hug Tony as soon as he entered.

"Tony, you look so much better now!" Arvind said happily as he rummaged around Tony's kitchen to find ingredients for tea. "But I am very upset that you never returned my calls. I was worried. By the way, there's so much I have to tell you. Eleena and I have decided to get married next year. I am planning to propose to her at Christmas, or maybe New Year's Day."

When the tea was ready, he brought it to the sofa and realized that Tony hadn't been listening to anything he had said.

"Hey," Arvind clicked his finger in front of Tony's face to bring him out of his slumber. "Are you okay, Tony? What happened?" he asked, anxious.

"I found Nancy," Tony said and was about to go back into the state of torpor when Arvind clicked his fingers again and this time Tony shoved his hand away, irritated.

"So? Who is she? And where is she?"

"Right here in Marsti, in our office." Tony said looking at Arvind whose face changed comically, tea held at lips, he went from being mildly curious to astonished as the gravity of that one simple sentence sunk in.

This time Tony clicked his fingers and nodded a yes.

"I need a drink," Arvind said and went to get a bottle of whiskey from Tony's kitchen as tony looked on, not surprised by his usually sober friend's desire to get drunk.

"Arvind, I need to speak to Leslie alone. I think I will drop in at the police station tomorrow," Tony said.

"Why don't you just call her?"

"Because I don't want to spook her, and if the murderer is someone close to her, then I don't want to warn him."

"Who could it be though, Tony?"'

"I don't know. The only logical person could be her husband, Thomas, but I don't think it's him. And in the last eight or nine months, I have not seen her mingle with people much. She has always been like this. There hasn't been anyone in her life apart from Thomas, not even friends. But I can't believe that it's Thomas.

"Tony, the man is a bisexual who had an affair with a pedophile. He could be our guy."

"Nope. I don't think it is. This is someone else who is closely linked to Leslie, somehow. That is why it's important that the meeting is set up impromptu, so that no one, not even Leslie doubts anything."

"Well, I might be able to arrange that then? Choose an option, my house, or El's, or the Town Hall?"

"The Town Hall. It will be crowded and loud enough that no one will hear us, but at the same time, I might be able to observe if someone is tailing Leslie. She could, herself, be in danger, if she does not know the killer."

"Okay. So then I will ask Eleena to invite her tomorrow to the Town Hall.

12th November
Saturday evening

Leslie and Eleena reach forty-five minutes after Arvind and Tony. They were waiting at the bar. Arvind, as decided, had told Eleena to invite Leslie for dinner with Arvind and Tony under the guise of celebrating Tony's return and a late Deepavali party from Arvind's side. Leslie had readily agreed, and had apologized that Thomas was busy with some important work, and would not be able to join them.

Tony wanted to talk to Leslie immediately, but he didn't. Tony's heart went out to the little girl Leslie had been, and the pain and trauma she had endured at the hands of the man she must have seen as her only family after her parents passed away.

Tony wanted to comfort her like he hadn't been able to his own daughter, but held back.

"Hi Leslie, hello Eleena. You both look beautiful!" Tony said and both looked taken aback. Tony hadn't spoken so happily and with such charm in ages.

Instead of going straight for dinner, Tony suggested they all have a drink at the bar.

"Leslie, do you dance?" Tony asked when their drinks had been served.

Leslie looked as if someone had pulled the carpet from under her, "No sir..." she muttered in a small voice.

"Oh, what kind of music do you like?"

Arvind and Eleena were looking at Tony and Leslie, and at each other. Tony asking Leslie for a dance was shocking to the point of being scandalous for them. And was he flirting with her? Arvind wondered inspite of knowing why Tony was interested in talking to Leslie because even he hadn't expected the conversation to go this way.

"How many drinks are you guys down?" Eleena asked Arvind softly.

"Just one beer each." Arvind whispered back in her ears, watching Tony, amused.

Tony went on to ask Leslie about her hobbies, if she watched movies, her favourite actor, if she read. Arvind and Eleena kept quiet, observing the interested queries of Tony and the shy, monosyllabic but polite answers of Leslie.

After a while, they proceeded to the dining hall and the dinner was much the same. Oblivious to not only strange looks from his own but other tables as well, Tony was focused on Leslie throughout the night.

After dinner, Tony offered to drop Leslie. When Eleena said she could, "Don't be silly! Leslie's house is on the way to my home. I will drop her and tomorrow I will drop Arvind's car," Tony said cheerfully.

Leslie muttered a thank you when Tony opened the car door for her and looked as if she would start crying any minute.

"What is up with Tony!? Is he okay? Has he lost his mind!?" Eleena almost shouted when Tony had driven away.

In the car, Tony switched off the music system and started making small talk as if to keep her entertained.

"Where is Thomas?"

"He is at home. He had some important work."

"Did you enjoy the evening?"

"Yes."

"How is work?"

"Good."

"Leslie, I never asked you, where did you work before you transferred here? Which chowki?"

"Tiruchirappalli, Chowki number 8."

"Oh! That's nice. It's a beautiful city, no? I was there recently."

Leslie had seemed tensed during dinner too, but now Tony saw the veins in her neck and forehead throbbing, but she didn't answer.

"How was it working in Tiruchirappalli?"

"Okay."

"You got married there too!"

"Yes."

"How was your wedding?"

"Okay." Tony looked at Leslie again, she wasn't sounding soft and shy anymore; her voice was almost harsh. He thought she was upset and wanted to console her.

"Leslie, it's okay. Your secret is safe with me. I understand."

Leslie just looked at Tony and when Tony took his eyes off of the road to reassure Leslie, he had to do a double take; some kind of change had come over her face. A change Tony couldn't place under any particular emotion.

Her usually hunched back was straight, her eyes too shiny. All the colour had left her face and she looked ashen, apart from her cheeks which were turning from pink to red and then an ugly purple, and her clenched jaw made her face look less cubby and more angular.

"Leslie, I am not trying to upset you. If you don't want to talk about it, we don't have to."

"Okay."

"But if we could talk, it might help me with Sam's case."

"No."

"No!? Leslie, you could help me catch my daughter's killer. These rapes and murders, they all may be related. You have to help me," Tony pleaded now.

"These?" she asked emotionlessly. The harshness in her voice so prominent that it barely sounded like her.

"Yes, I can't tell you much right now, but my investigation suggests we might have a serial killer on our hands. Help me, Leslie. I know it must be painful for you, but you are a woman, you must understand!"

"No," Leslie replied with finality, and a shocked and angry Tony increased the speed of the car.

"Nancy Damascus, I am trying to save you too. Help me help you."

"My house is close now. I would like to walk the rest of the way home," Leslie replied curtly.

"It's okay. It's too late to walk. I will drop you home," Tony said through gritted teeth.

"No. I want to get down here. Stop the car."

Tony had no option but to stop the car and let her alight.

Tony had expected that when he asked her about her past, she would cry, or break down, but Tony couldn't make sense of this 360 degree behavioural change in her.

13th November
Sunday

Tony called Leslie, but she kept disconnecting his call.

Tony called Thomas and asked to meet him at David's bar.

"Why did you want to meet me this time, Tony? Are you going to arrest me again?" Thomas asked huffily before taking a seat next to Tony. Dressed in a white polo T-shirt and dark blue jeans, Thomas looked sophisticated.

"Not at all, Thomas. I don't have a grudge against you. In fact, you remember I tried talking to you, but you refused to talk without an arrest warrant. What was I supposed to do?" Tony said calmly.

"Why did you want to meet me?" Thomas asked shortly.

"I wanted to ask you to let bygones be bygones. We live in a small town and we shouldn't be enemies. I have always admired you, you know, for your sharp dressing sense and grooming. And then this whole thing happened. Shall we forget the episode and start a fresh as friends?"

Thomas smiled.

"Let me buy you a beer," Tony said slapping Thomas on the back

"Well, I am not a beer man, but a Corona should be okay," Thomas said, adjusting his Rolex watch, trying to draw Tony's attention to it.

"So, how is business? Flourishing, I am sure!" Tony said positively after placing the order.

"Oh, the festive seasons are always good. A jeweller's success or failure is defined by how well he does during off season. But I have just opened up. The best part is there isn't any competition here."

"No?" Tony asked surprised, "but we have Thakkar's shop."

"Ah! He is no competition to me. The man couldn't sell a camel in the desert. He is a bad businessman. One needs to understand what the customer needs. That is the key, always."

"Of course. What competition could a small town jeweller pose to a man who has run a successful business in a big city like Tiruchirappalli?"

"Exactly! And I didn't have competition there either! In fact, I have wondered since shifting here if this was a good idea."

"I agree! Why did you shift here anyway?"

"I thought business here would be more peaceful. As much as I enjoy a healthy competition, it kept me away from my passions too often. And I guess Leslie is happy here, too. Not that she ever complained in Tiruchirappalli. And it's not like she has a real job, anyway, so she would be happy anywhere."

"Yes buddy, I mean a jeweller's wife, a constable! And believe me, I have never seen a more mismatched pair than the two of you," Tony said jovially. "Yours is an arranged marriage, right?"

"Not at all! It was a love marriage, through and through. Leslie doesn't have any family and my parents are settled abroad after separating. Honestly, if I had met Leslie directly for marriage, like a set up by relatives or parents or friends, I would have rejected her right off the bat!"

"True. There is no match. But how did you two end up together then?"

"Oh, I was planning on putting up another shop and had gone to see some properties in Chennai. It was my college friend's daughter's naming ceremony and she insisted that I come. I met Leslie at that party. So there I was sipping my soft drink, and wishing for Bourbon, when I saw Leslie. My friend's husband is an officer and Leslie was his colleague. To pass time, I went up to Leslie and started a conversation. And that was it," he said nonchalant.

"I still don't understand why. I mean, don't get me wrong bro, but she seems so shy and you are so charming, she is awkward and you are so confident. I get it that she is a sweet natured girl, but I still don't understand how a man like you would fall in love with a girl like her."

"Tony, my boy, love is overrated. And a wife doesn't need to be beautiful or charming to be a good housekeeper. She has to be mild and unquestioning. I married Leslie because she doesn't interfere in my life. She gives me my space. I don't need a wife with a mouth. When I met Leslie, I knew that this was a woman who would never open her trap other than to put food in it," Thomas said and laughed aloud.

"Oh. That is very smart buddy!"

"Of course. So I met Leslie a few times and was almost going to ask her to marry me, but then she told me she didn't want to have children, and that sealed the deal, because I hate kids!"

"That's most clever Thomas. Cheers to that!" Tony raised his beer bottle and downed it and Thomas followed suit. Tony ordered another round and told the bartender to keep the beer coming. "We are celebrating our new friendship!"

"But don't you get bored of her antisocial behaviour? Was she like this when you met her?" Tony asked, taking a big gulp from his second Corona bottle.

"No! She was worse! In five years of my marriage, I haven't seen her make a single friend. But when I met her, she would get sick at the thought of meeting people. She is worse than anti-social – a loner. She doesn't watch TV and doesn't even have a Facebook or Instagram account! Her only form of entertainment is her workout sessions. She has nightmares where she starts thrashing in bed violently. The works!"

"Work out and Leslie!? You must be joking!" Tony asked surprised.

"Dude, you have no idea. She spends hours at the gym in our house. And then she runs for miles. Her stamina is commendable, really. Under all those baggy clothes is quite a toned and strong body. She could give tough competition to a man your size!"

"I don't believe it!" Tony said.

"Well, there's no way to prove to you, anyway. She refuses to wear anything but her baggy clothes. This has been one thing about her that gets under my skin. But she keeps my house clean and my bed warm. But believe me, this woman is pure naked muscle power."

"And what nightmares?"

"Oh... I dont know really. I asked her when we were newly married, but she said she doesn't remember. I had asked if she wanted to see a doctor, she said no, so it must not be serious."

"What do you mean violent nightmares?"

"Well... she starts throwing her hands around. She seems to struggle in these dreams. And she mutters something too."

"What?" Tony asked concerned.

"God knows! I never paid much attention. Whenever she is having a bad night, I sleep in the guest room. It's quite nice sleeping alone, sometimes." He said upraising Tony, eyes resting for a few seconds longer than needed on his nether regions. "I can watch porn when I am alone. Not that Leslie would say anything if I watched it in front of her," Thomas said winking.

"Can I ask you something, buddy? If you don't mind?"

"Not at all. Go ahead."

"It sounds like nothing you do bothers this woman. Are you sure she loves you? Tell me, did she fight with you when your sexuality came out?" Tony whispered confidentially.

"Leslie always knew I was bisexual. She had walked in on me and a guy one day when she came home early from work because she was feeling sick."

"Oh god! She must have beaten the shit out of you!"

"On the contrary, she politely closed the door, went and took a bath in the guest bedroom of our Tiruchirappalli bungalow, and made dinner," Thomas said quietly, smiling.

"That's why I said, does she love you, Thomas?"

"Who cares? She is not the kind to cheat, and my sexual interests don't bother her. So it really doesn't matter."

"How can you be so sure that she wouldn't cheat? You have cheated on her."

"Because she hates sex," he said slyly smiling as if sharing a joke. "In fact, when I want to have sex with her, it's really just wham bam thank you ma'am. She doesn't moan or react. Just lays there like a dead body."

"Hey, excuse me buddy, nature's call, be right back." Tony excused himself, unable to hold back his rage at Thomas's shallow and superficial mindset.

He had come close to punching his teeth in quite a few times, but had controlled his anger. He couldn't control the empathy and sorrow that was rising in his heart for Leslie's condition. Splashing water on his face, he returned with a wide smile.

"Ufff! It stinks in there!"

Subtly, Thomas placed a casual hand on Tony's thigh and then started to move his fingers up and down his legs. Tony, when he couldn't bear anymore, took Thomas's hand in his own, held it calmly, still talking and smiling, he started to slowly exert pressure on his fingers. After about thirty seconds, Thomas himself pulled his hand away, rubbing the fingers and didn't try again that night.

14th November
Monday

Tony kept trying Leslie's cell phone, every half an hour, and she kept disconnecting the calls. He finally called the police station number, but Leslie hung up as soon as Tony said hello. He decided to go and meet her in the evening.

Pervez Sheikh called at noon.

"I have found two more cases in Chennai, but none in Bangalore, and yet again, you will have to come yourself to collect the files," he said and explained the details which Tony noted down.

"Tony, I still suggest you speak to the DCP, instead of trying to find this man yourself," Pervez advised before hanging up.

At 07.00 p.m., Tony reached the police station to talk to Leslie, but Arvind told him that she had left early, saying she wasn't well.

Tony again called her, but she didn't answer.

Tony called Thomas to ask him what he and Leslie were doing for the night and Thomas said he was at home. "What do you want to do?" Thomas asked, "I am getting bored at home and Leslie is also working late tonight. You haven't seen my house, have you? Come over here or I can come over? Should I get beer?"

"Oh! Working late at the police station?"

"Dude! Where else will she work? So, your place or mine?"

"Wait a minute, oh, I am getting a call. Let me call you back, Thomas," Tony said and hung up.

"Leslie might be involved with the killer, Arvind," Tony said somberly.

"How can you say that? Did Thomas say something?"

"She lied to Thomas about working late tonight. What time did she leave the station?"

"Around 3.30. But she really was sick. She puked after lunch. I could hear her loud retches from the bathroom till my desk!"

Tony got into his car and drove to Thomas's house, picking beer on the way, and dropping Arvind at Eleena's. Thomas was happily surprised to see Tony and called a restaurant to order snacks and dinner.

At 10.35 p.m., Leslie opened the door with her own keys, called out to Thomas. She stood looking shocked when she saw Tony in her living room. She recovered, but not quickly enough. Tony had noticed the dismay in her face. And fear maybe? Thomas saw nothing amiss. He smiled up at her, and returned his attention to pouring beer in their tall glasses.

"How was your day? I have ordered some food for me and Tony. Will you be having dinner?"

"I am not feeling well," she said rubbing her forehead. "I will have a shower and go to sleep. You continue please," and walked away up the stairs to her room.

"Please don't mind. She has been over-working herself lately. It's irritating to see her so tired every day, but she refuses to quit," Thomas said, remote in his hand, changing TV channels with one hand and sipping his beer.

Tony left Thomas's house soon after and called Arvind from the car.

"Leslie lied to Thomas about being at work. But she was elsewhere. We have to find out where she goes when she is not at home or at work. I have a plan and I will need your help for it. But Arvind, it will take away a lot of your personal time that you may want to spend with Eleena."

"Please Anna! Just tell me what you need from me. Anything for you!"

"Okay. We are going to keep an eye on Leslie. It might be a little difficult, but liars, especially people who lie regularly, always have a pattern to their lies. I need you to look out for these deceptions."

"I didn't understand that part, Tony. What am I supposed to look out for?" Arvind asked.

"She left work today at 3.30 in the afternoon and reached home post 10.30 p.m. She lied at work and at home. This can't be the only time she's done this. I remember her asking for leaves a few times before I was suspended. So next time she says she is not well or starts to behave like she is sick, I want you to call me immediately. But between the time she starts to act sick and then finally leaves, she will do the pretending and the lying. I want you to observe how she behaves, what she does, precisely, every time."

"Huh? You want me to tell you how she behaves other than behaving sick?"

"I want to know how many times she goes to the bathroom, what she ate, everything! Note it down if you have to, of course, not at the cost of your duty. But observe everything she does and doesn't do and report it back to me. Okay?"

"Okay Tony."

"And, this one is the difficult one. I need the attendance books for the last six months."

Arvind replied after a long pause, "Sorry, I was just trying to remember where the attendance rosters are kept. The current one is kept in your cabin and the old ones are in the store room. The old ones will not be difficult to get out, but the current one will be. Let me figure out how to get it."

"For the current register, you can also take picture of each page, and Whatsapp it to me."

"That's perfect. I will try to see if I can do it tomorrow itself."

"If she doesn't leave early tomorrow, let me know. I will come to the police station at 7.00 and try to talk to her again."

15th November
Tuesday

Arvind called Tony at 5.00 p.m. when he saw that Leslie was not pretending to be sick or unwell. Tony reached the police station and waited outside. At 7.15 Leslie came out, followed by Arvind.

Tony got out of the car as Leslie was walking towards the rickshaw stand that was a ten minute walk away. She stopped mid-step when she saw Tony and then started walking faster, almost running.

"Hey, I just want to talk, Leslie. Wait! Stop!" But Leslie didn't stop and Tony, irritated, took a few long steps and held Leslie by her arm, just above the elbow, turning her around.

"Why won't you talk to me? I feel bad for you. What happened to you was wrong. But you should be helping me find this killer yourself. Because you know the pain that my daughter went through. Then why are you refusing to even talk to me?" Tony asked, angry and emotional, because of the helplessness he was feeling.

"Leave my hand!" Leslie spat. Her face set in stone, eyes glaring, spitting fire. And Tony was a little more than surprised to feel the bulging muscles in her flexing arm.

"Please Leslie, at least tell me why you don't want to talk. Is it because it will be painful? I know it will be, but you will feel better once you know that a killer has been punished for it. Or is it because you are scared of someone? I can help you, Leslie. Please. Let me help you," Tony finished, almost pleading.

"Leave my hand!" Leslie said and jerked her hand out with an aggression he hadn't expected. Tony took a step back, looking at her as if seeing her for the first time. Arvind, watching everything from a few steps away till now, ran towards Tony and looked from Tony to Leslie, equally surprised.

"If you try to talk to me again, I will complain to the commissioner that you are stalking me. I will charge you with sexual harassment. And I mean it. Leave me alone, or I will make your life a living hell," she said through clenched teeth, her finger pointing at his chest. Instead of the fumbling, awkward woman, she stood tall over the two of them. "And stay away from Thomas and my house too. Got it?" she said and walked away, her body language confident.

For a good ten minutes, Tony and Arvind sat in the car, absolutely quiet. Arvind was trying to play down what he had seen, but was finding it difficult to underplay the fact that a woman, who till a few hours ago was seen as a poor little miss, had suddenly turned into a vicious woman who was threatening Tony.

"I had a busy day, so couldn't get the attendance register," he said trying to change the subject, but Tony didn't reply. He looked like he was calculating something and then he went blank again.

"What the hell is wrong with this girl? Is she mad? Bloody psycho! Why won't she talk? You should do as Pervez sir is saying, Tony," Arvind said finally, frustrated at Tony's helplessness.

"Arvind, you are brilliant! We need a psychiatrist, someone who can evaluate Leslie."

"Tony, if she won't talk to you, what makes you think she will talk to a shrink? Why are you so hell bent on trying to help someone who refuses to help us? And she behaved so weirdly back there."

"Arvind, don't you have an uncle in Pondicherry who is a psychiatrist?"

"Yes. But he retired a few years back. Why?"

"Can you call and ask him if he can come to Marsti?"

"Oh... Yes." Arvind said as he finally understood what Tony was saying. He called his uncle, Dr M. Shrinivasan.

"He will be here by tomorrow afternoon, Tony. He was most happy to hear I am getting married and agreed immediately. He thinks I am calling him to get his approval of Eleena."

"Now see if Eleena can invite Leslie at your place for dinner tomorrow. No. She knows you are close to me and after what she's done in front of you, she might say she's busy. Tell Eleena to call Leslie to her own place to meet her uncle."

"I will call her..."

"No. Speak to her face to face, and Arvind, tell her why we are doing this. If she is going to help us, then she needs to know the gravity and risk of helping us. We have to be careful. Very, very careful."

"Careful of what, Tony?"

"Just be careful. Call me and let me know what happens. And also the time at which I should come to your house to meet your uncle." Tony dropped Arvind at Eleena's place and went home.

16th November
Wednesday

Arvind called Tony late morning to request him to go to his house, to keep his uncle company and update him about Leslie. He was unable to leave early because of the work load, but promised to get the attendance register in the evening.

Tony disconnected the call and dialled Leslie's number, yet again, and as Tony expected, she disconnected it. Tony sent her a message which read, "I will find the killer, whether you help me or not."

When it showed that the message was read, Tony tried calling Leslie again, but her phone was unreachable.

"Hi, where are you? Did uncle reach alright?" Arvind asked when he called Tony in the afternoon.

"Yes. Your neighbour had opened the door for him with your keys before I reached. He was rummaging your fridge when I came. I have ordered some food for us. What time are you getting done?"

"I don't know. There was a fight on Church Street between two tourists. I will try and come as soon as possible. Oh, by the way, Eleena messaged sometime back; she managed to persuade Leslie to meet her this evening under the ruse that she was going to break the wedding news to her uncle and needed a friend by her side. Apparently Leslie had other plans, but El managed to convince her."

"What other plans? Did she say?"

"No. But she got sick sometime back. In fact, just after I spoke to you in the morning, she rushed to the toilet and then I heard her shout. When I knocked on the door, she said she had just dropped her phone. But she hasn't said anything about leaving early as yet."

"How much time after you spoke to me?" Tony asked curiously.

"Oh, about five minutes or so. Why?

"Keep an eye on her. Don't forget to call me the minute she starts playing the 'not feeling well' card again."

"Tony, I think she was sick. I saw her face; it was pale and she was sweating and her phone, when she came out, was broken."

"Arvind, I had messaged her after I spoke to you. I will tell you everything in the evening. After lunch I will tell your uncle why exactly we need him."

Arvind's uncle was a jolly man with quick wit and a flamboyant attitude towards life. At seventy, he walked with a spring in his steps, spoke about music like it was wine, and advised Tony to stay off alcohol and cigarettes, out of the blue.

The man dressed in a formal shirt and pants, with a thinning head of hair, bright smile and husky voice, made his place in Tony's heart by his openness, kindness, and humour.

After lunch, Tony told the old doctor about his daughter, his search, the gut feeling that took him across three cities in Tamil Nadu and the series of murders he had uncovered and their link to a constable in his own town. Dr Shrinivasan heard everything in silence, amazed and horrified.

When Tony had finished talking, Dr Shrinivasan got himself a glass of water, drank it, looking at Tony over the rim of the glass. He put the empty glass on the tea table and lay down on the sofa in the living area. He fell asleep soon after and not knowing what to do, Tony switched on the TV.

The doorbell woke them both and Tony opened to door to let Arvind in. Arvind was happy to see his uncle after three years. Both exchanged some pleasantries and uncle again went back to lie on the sofa.

When Arvind saw this, he asked Tony what was wrong.

"I told uncle everything," he said simply and shrugged, not knowing what was going on in his uncle's mind. He started flipping through the attendance registers Arvind had dumped on the sofa.

Arvind turned to his uncle, who finally smiled and sat up.

"What time are we going for dinner to my niece Eleena's place? And I will need to know more about her than her name, if I am to pretend to be her uncle!" he said, grinning and then winked at them both.

"Arvind, keep an eye out for anything out of ordinary and reach before Leslie does, so that you can hide in the house in a room. I will see if Leslie's leaves give us a pattern," Tony said, reassured that he had the help of an experienced doctor.

Arvind and Dr Shrinivasan reached at 7.30 p.m. and Arvind hid in Eleena's room when Leslie rang the doorbell. Both Eleena and Arvind's uncle had come up with a fake history about their relationship.

"Is Arvind here?" Leslie asked as soon as she came in, looking around. Eleena noticed that she seemed different. Alert. On guard.

"No. Why?"

"I saw his car on the street," she said looking suspiciously at Eleena, and then seeing Dr Shrinivasan, she tried to smile. In the room, Arvind slapped his forehead at the mistake.

"Oh, I borrowed his car. Mine has a battery problem. He is at home. Did you want to meet him?" Eleena said, unperturbed, impressing Arvind who was listening from inside the bedroom.

"No. Hello," Leslie said to Arvind's uncle and they proceeded to the dining area.

The talk started off with Eleena telling Dr Shrinivasan about Leslie and what a great friend she had become of Eleena's in a short period of time. And the pleasantries continued while Eleena started laying the table. Arvind and his uncle had decided that they would not bring up Dr Shrinivasan's profession as that might put Leslie on guard. When Leslie asked what Dr Shrinivasan's job was, he said he was a retired professor of biology.

"My Eleena was very poor at studies growing up. How about you, darling? Where did you go to school?" Dr Shrinivasan asked at the chance to question Leslie.

"In Chennai," she said.

"I stayed in Chennai for a few years when I was younger," he said smiling. "Did you like growing up in a big city like that?"

"Hmmm..."

"That's nice. It really doesn't matter where one grows up. It's the upbringing that really matters at the end of the day. Eleena was a complete spoiled brat. How about you? Did you give your parents a lot of trouble too?" he asked lightly.

"No." Leslie said shortly. "So, have you fixed a date for your wedding yet, Eleena?" she tried changing the subject.

"No, we haven't set a date yet, but it will be January or February of next year, hopefully. Did you have a lavish reception, Leslie? You could help me with mine. We are thinking of a church wedding," Eleena asked.

"A church wedding? That's preposterous! Arvind can't get married in a church; he is a Hindu! The wedding will be a traditional ceremony with all the rituals and customs followed to the T." Dr Shrinivasan said sternly before Leslie could reply, forgetting the situation for the moment.

"Eleena is a Christian. Are you Hindu, Dr Shrinivasan?" Leslie asked, eyes intent, looking at Eleena and her uncle.

"He is my mother's brother. She was a Hindu. You know how orthodox people can get about all these things," Eleena said smoothly, rolling her eyes at Dr Shrinivasan, who was getting his act under control. "We will have a traditional Hindu wedding, if that's what you want, Uncle Shri. Arvind and I really don't care as long as we are together," she told Dr Shrinivasan, and he looked impressed with his nephew's choice.

Leslie was looking at both suspiciously.

"So, was your wedding a grand affair?" Dr Shrinivasan asked.

"No. I had a court marriage," she said shortly.

"Oh! And your parents didn't have a problem with that?" Dr Shrinivasan enquired, eating his curd rice with pickle.

"My parents died when I was six."

"That's very sad to hear, darling," Dr Shrinivasan said genuinely and reached across the table to hold Leslie's hand in comfort and as she suddenly jerked her hand away, her fingers brushed the glass of juice and it smashed on the floor, stunning everyone.

"I am sorry," Leslie said, but glared angrily at Dr Shrinivasan for just a moment and cast her eyes away as soon as he looked at her. But not before he had noticed the stare and the way she was trying to wipe the hand he had touched on her dress, like it was soiled. She tried smiling and failed this time and asked where the bathroom was.

"Sorry, I can be very clumsy sometimes," Leslie said when she returned. The glass had been cleared away by Eleena.

"So, who did you stay with after your parents?" Dr Shrinivasan asked.

"My uncle."

"Oh! Was he a good man? Was he married?" asked Dr Shrinivasan, observing her keenly.

"Eleena, I am not feeling well. I think I will go home now. Sorry," Leslie said, getting up and grabbing her purse.

"Can't you stay for a little longer? You haven't even had dessert! I had ordered almond caramel cake from Franco's bakery!"

"No. I don't like sweets and I am feeling nauseous. I had a great time, Eleena. It was good to meet you Dr Shrinivasan," she said, taking her purse and keys and walking towards the door.

"I will have Uncle Shri drop you. He is diabetic and can't have sweets too."

"He might get lost on the way back," she said without a smile and looked at Dr Shrinivasan. "You should take it easy, Uncle Shri, at your age," she said and was gone.

"I need to talk to Tony," Dr Shrinivasan said to Arvind who had come out of the room as soon as Leslie left.

Quickly, they got into Arvind's car and drove to his house, where Tony was waiting eagerly.

"She had taken a half day the day Sam went missing," Tony said as soon as they entered.

"Tony, the dinner didn't go as planned. She got upset and left before uncle could get anything out of her," Arvind told Tony.

"Yes. She did leave before I could get any useful information, but I did learn something about your friend," Dr Shrinivasan said seriously.

"Arvind, Tony, you guys are looking at only her history, but have either of you tried to find out about her mental health?"

"What do you mean, uncle?" Arvind asked.

"There wasn't much to find out there. The court had put her through sessions with a doctor to help and evaluate her state during the trail, but it doesn't say much other than she was traumatized and was recovering. Her principal at junior college had tried to counsel her, but he too thought she was alright. But there was an incident. She had broken a boy's finger in college when he had tried to kiss her on a date," Tony replied.

"Hmmm... I thought as much. She has a violent streak. She hides it well. But it's there. And she also pretends to behave a certain way, but her eyes give her away. Tell me how she is at work and how she is otherwise. Have you guys noticed any difference in her behaviour when she is under stress?"

Tony and Arvind looked at each other in surprise. They had been shocked at her behaviour the previous evening. They told Dr Shrinivasan about the incident and how far apart her behaviour had been from how she usually was.

"She may be dangerous. I don't know if she is helping someone or if she is even related to your investigation, Tony, though I have a feeling she may be, but she has a very prominent violent streak. When I touched her hand, she looked at me like she wanted to kill me. I have only ever seen such behaviour in very few patients who have a tendency to harm themselves or others."

"Harm themselves? You mean she could hurt herself?"

"Yes. But from whatever you have told me so far, it doesn't sound like she has ever done anything harmful to herself. But she had physically hurt this boy. Are you sure there hasn't been any other incident like that?"

"No. I am not sure. But most of the people who I spoke to said she was a demure girl, and an awkward and clumsy woman. A quiet woman."

"She is not quiet, Tony. She is secretive. There is a difference. I believe the reason she doesn't talk is because she doesn't want to reveal anything, either about herself or something in her life."

"But will you be able to make her talk? It's important to find her link to all the murders," Tony asked, desperately.

"I can try. But honestly, she's too careful and guarded. I can't promise, my child. Sorry. But I will try. I need to meet her a few more times. Is it possible?"

Over the next two days, Dr Shrinivasan went everywhere Leslie was. Eleena took him to the police station, purposely leaving home after Arvind to pretend that they were both coming separately. She told Arvind, within Leslie's earshot that she couldn't take Uncle Shri to the hospital with her, so Arvind would have to look after him till evening.

Dr Shrinivasan tried talking to Leslie at the police station, but she said she had a headache and talking hurt even more, ending any chance of conversation. Not one to be put off easily, Dr Shrinivasan rummaged through the police station first aid kit and took out a Crocin for her.

"I don't take medication for small things like a headache. I just need to stay quiet and it will pass over. Thank you," Leslie said formally, dismissing Dr Shrinivasan with finality.

After that, he decided to just observe her. The doctor noticed Leslie was uncomfortable at being watched constantly by him, and knew that she was pretending to not notice and behave indifferent.

On the second evening, when Eleena came to pick up the old doctor, Leslie was leaving too. Eleena asked her to have a coffee at the tea stall outside the police station. Leslie said she was getting late, but when Eleena told her that she was trying to set Tony up with a girl from her hospital and needed her advice, Leslie agreed to talk while they had some tea.

"Oh, this girl I have known from my childhood. We were in the same school and she has recently shifted to Marsti. She is a doctor too," Eleena laughed.

Tony and Dr Shrinivasan had come to the conclusion that Leslie's mental issues were rooted in her childhood and prepared Eleena on what to say and how. Laughing and joking, Eleena started yapping about her childhood and that is when Dr Shrinivasan observed the change in Leslie's demeanour. Leslie was looking at her feet while Eleena talked. Then she started talking about her Uncle Shri putting her to bed every night, reading stories, giving her baths, and taking her to school. Tony had picked that bit of Garry Damascus's routine from her Aunt Ruth. Suddenly, a barrage of emotions started running across her face. She tried to control it, but couldn't. She was not looking at her feet anymore. She was mouthing something silently. This time Dr Shrinivasan knew what he was seeing clearly.

"Leslie definitely is still carrying the seed of her childhood trauma in her mind. She has depression and there is a definite chance that she may be suffering from some other disorders too."

"You mean she is mad?" Arvind asked and Eleena slapped his arm.

"Don't be such a dud! Every person who has an emotional or mental issue is not mad. Most of these disorders are curable. That is why we put them in hospitals and not jail!" Eleena said austerely.

"Yes. She is right, Arvind. You have got yourself a smart girl. But dear Eleena, some mental disorders are dangerous and sometimes incurable. I am not saying that is the case with Leslie. But her issues are very deep rooted and have been persistently growing over a long time. Unless she speaks to me freely, I can't say if her issues are curable or not."

"What exactly do you think she has, Uncle Shri?" Tony asked somberly.

"This is my understanding so far and I am not sure, but I think Leslie has what we call Dissociative Personality Disorder or Bipolar Disorder."

Eleena and Tony listened attentively while Arvind removed his phone and searched on Google.

"It's when a person, faced with extreme trauma or pain, creates an alter self. That person's personality or self gets divided into two or more identities. Each identity is separate from the other, as different as each of you are from each other. These alter selves sometimes know each other and sometimes they don't. They may even be enemies of each other," Dr Shrinivasan said to the three people looking up at him with rapt attention.

"I don't understand. I had read an article about Multiple Personality Disorder but what is Bipolar Disorder then?"

"Simply put, bipolar disorder has more to do with the behavioural changes in a person. People who have this cannot take charge of their emotions. Anger, depression, love, sadness, obsession, and every other emotion is on a spring, ready to jump out like a jack in the box."

"Oh. And she has both?"

"I didn't say that! I said she might. The thing is a person who has MPD disassociates herself or himself from the situation or themselves, to be able to bear the pain and ends up creating alter egos to deal with the pain. BD is only related to a person's inability to deal with their own extreme feelings. Leslie may have both or either or neither. Again, chances are, I might be wrong."

"Is she capable of being involved in kidnappings or murders?" Tony asked anxiously.

"Her alter ego or other personalities within her might be."

When Leslie reached home, Thomas was lying on the bed, naked. She undressed, got into bed without saying anything and switched off the bedside lamp. Thomas came over her and Leslie shut her eyes. After a couple of minutes, a heaving Thomas got off Leslie, turned around, said good night. He was snoring in five minutes.

Leslie got out of the bed, hand on mouth, breathing heavy herself, she went into the bathroom and closed the door. She opened the shower and the washbasin tap and finally removing the hand from her mouth, puked the dinner out. She got into the shower, and began vigorously rubbing soap over her while the hot water cascaded over her head, her rounded breast, her flat, muscled stomach, her thick shapely thighs. She stood in the shower till the water ran cold, and bar of soap had almost dissolved, and her tears had dried out in her wet eyes.

19th November
Saturday

"Tony, Leslie hasn't come to work today. Where are you?"

"I know. I am outside her house. I came here last night from your house and in time too. She went for a jog around 2.00 a.m. I followed her, but lost her near sunset point. Thomas was right, he had said that Leslie loves running and so she does, and fast. For a big woman, she sure is agile. She returned around 4.30 a.m." Tony said yawning.

"Have you slept at all?"

"Not really. Listen, you won't be able to take an off. Do you mind asking Uncle Shri to help me, if he is not too tired, in keeping a watch on Leslie's house? That way we won't miss her if I fall asleep."

"Yes. Of course. And Tony, after what uncle said last night, I am worried. Be careful."

Uncle Shri called Tony back after ten minutes to tell him that he had taken a rickshaw towards Leslie's house following the GPS location Tony had sent. Tony told him to leave the rickshaw exactly at the location, right next to his black Santro. Tony had brought out his wife's old car from the garage and was parked some distance away.

They spent the whole day watching Leslie's house, one sleeping while the other kept surveillance, but she didn't step out. At around 7.15 p.m., Thomas came home, and after another half hour, Thomas and Leslie got into his car and drove out. Tony tailed them to the Town Hall. Dr Shrinivasan, having eaten only a sandwich for late breakfast, suggested they go inside and watch her while having dinner instead of waiting in the car, hungry.

They sat at the bar, inconspicuously, and ordered tandoori chicken. When Leslie noticed Tony, she walked out. Tony left Dr Shrinivasan at the bar and followed her discreetly. She was walking towards the parking lot; he hid from her behind a Maruti Swift when she turned around.

Tony decided to try and talk to Leslie again if he got the chance, but kept his distance for the time being.

"So..." Leslie said, "here I am Tony. What do you want to do?" she had come up behind Tony. He hadn't realized when she had sneaked back. Legs apart, hands folded across her broad chest, a look of annoyance and impatience on her face. Dressed in a plain dark blue salwar kameez, bindi on her forehead, devoid of makeup, hair tied in a bow; her body language didn't match her attire in the least.

"I don't want anything but to talk to you, Leslie."

"I told you I have nothing to say to you. Why don't you leave me alone?" she asked serenely.

"Because I can't. You are the only one who can help me. And I know you are hiding something. Why don't you want to talk? At least tell me that."

"Will you leave me alone then?"

"No, I can't. But it will be one mystery solved if you tell me what or who is stopping you from talking to me."

"And what will you do if I refuse to speak?"

"I don't have to do anything. The police and court will decide your fate then, Leslie. Or should I call you Nancy? Or Emma?"

"Names don't matter to me; you must know that by now."

"Really." Tony said, more as a statement than a question.

"What matters, Tony, is that you are wasting my time and becoming an unnecessary menace."

"How so?"

"I know you have nothing against me."

"I have everything against you, Leslie."

Leslie laughed. It was a friendly, pat on the back kind of laugh. Tony was taken aback to see her guffawing like that. He came to realize at that moment that Dr Shrinivasan's suspicion might be true.

Since joining work, he had known Leslie as a shy, scared, easily spooked woman. This woman who stood in front of him was confident, intelligent, and coldly calculative. Maybe she really knows I have nothing concrete, Tony thought, maybe she knows that all the evidence collected so far is only circumstantial.

"Cheers to that!" Tony said indulgingly, and raised the beer glass he held in his hand. Leslie was still smiling but the smile did not reach her eyes. It was more a show of teeth and stretch of facial muscles than humor or good nature.

"Tony, my dear, if you had anything, I would be dead or behind bars. I know you have suspicions, and you worked so hard..." she said mockingly.

"But now you have become a pain in my butt. So here goes. Yes. You are right. I am connected to your daughter's rape and murder. Wanna know how?" she asked almost jovially. At Sam's mention, Tony had started to hear her voices pleading for help again. He wasn't capable of saying anything and Leslie continued, "I killed Sam. But can you prove it?"

Tony was stunned. He now felt unsure of what was happening. He stood rooted to the spot, blinking his eyes as if clearing a fog in his mind. And Leslie started laughing again and this time she sounded like the killer from his nightmares.

"You bitch! What the fuck are you saying? I will kill you if you don't tell me who it is!" Tony was angry at Leslie's derisive tone and what she was saying. Tony was yelling and the people standing around the parking lot were starting to walk towards them.

"Who is who?" she laughed again.

"Stop laughing and tell me who it is!" Tony said sternly.

"Who is who? Who is who? Who is who?" Leslie started singing softly, while tears were flowing down her eyes and her face was contorted in fear and pain.

"What the fuck are you doing? Why are you doing this!?" Tony asked and Leslie's face changed dramatically at the question.

"Because I like it, sweetheart! And Sam liked it too, and so did all the other girls," Leslie replied. She was still speaking only for Tony's ears, but her voice had changed completely. It was husky and rough. Her whole demeanour had become manly.

Leslie looked Tony straight in the eyes and said, "I had a great time with Sammy. She was one of my best!" And suddenly Tony realized what Leslie was saying.

Leslie was *the killer!* Not an accomplice or a helper. She was the rapist and the murderer!

Tony put his hands around her neck, chocking Leslie, and she started shouted, "Help!" ear-piercingly.

"I will kill you, you bitch!" Tony was yelling now.

"Please Tony, don't hurt me. Please Tony. *Help me someone! Help me*!"

She was shrieking loudly as people gathered and started pulling Tony off. Leslie kicked him in his balls, missing him mostly, but hurting him enough that he let her go. Someone yelled at Leslie to get out of there.

"What is wrong with you, Tony? I can have you arrested for attacking a woman! Have you lost your mind?" Mrs Krishnan said, who had run over from her office on the second floor of the building. She had seen most of what had happened and didn't understand if Tony had finally lost his mind or if this was just another episode bought on by his continuous failure to solve his daughter's murder and alcohol.

"She is the killer." Tony said, unable to speak loud, still on his knees.

He watched as Leslie got in her car, smiling at Tony, with a flabbergasted Thomas who looked pale and scared for his life, and drove away.

Dr Shrinivasan had called Arvind as soon as he saw the confrontation. Now he kneeled next to Tony, trying to pick him up by arms, with the help of five other men.

Dr Shrinivasan drove a dazed Tony home. In pain, feeling nauseous at what Leslie had said, unbelieving of even the possibility that it was true, Tony just kept replaying the events as they had played out. He didn't say anything on the way. When Arvind called his uncle from on the way to the

Town Hall, Dr Shrinivasan told him to go back home and wait there.

"How is that even possible, Tony? You must be mistaken!" Arvind asked when Tony finally told them what had transpired.

"I don't know anymore. I find it hard to believe, but that is what she said. And that laugh!"

Dr Shrinivasan was sitting quietly, a look of trouble and dismay in his eyes. Eleena had just come out of the room she shared with Arvind, looking from one face to another; she felt sure that something terrible had happened.

"I think it is quite possible, and that means I was right in my assessment of her. She does have Disassociative Personality Disorder. One of her alter egos is that of a rapist," he said wretchedly.

"What!? What is happening, Arvind?" Eleena asked.

"We need to speak to Commissioner sir, Tony. We will show him all the evidence collected. They can take over then." Arvind said. Tony agreed and dialled the commissioner's mobile number, but it went unanswered.

"Please call me sir. It is urgent. Anthony George, Marsti Police station." Tony sent a message on the number.

They decided to wait for him to call back.

Arvind narrated the conversation that had taken place at the Town Hall to Eleena. Without speaking a word, she went to sit next to Dr Shrinivasan. She too, like Tony, Arvind, and the doctor was struggling with the gravity of the situation.

"So in short, Leslie is a madwoman who has a split personality of a pedophile serial killer!?" She said after sometime, but no one replied.

They all sat together in the hall, dozing in and out of sleep, waiting for the call from the commissioner.

20th November
Sunday

When Tony's phone finally rang in the morning, jerking out of his stupor, he picked it up immediately. It was a call from the commissioner. He had just introduced himself as Anthony George from Marsti Town, when the commissioner spoke.

"You are the suspended officer whose daughter passed away a few months ago?"

"Yes sir. And I have..."

"And you were suspended from duty soon after?"

"Yes sir," Tony said, self-consciously.

"Were you drinking on duty?"

"Sir, I had called to talk to you about Lady Constable Leslie Braganza. Sir, she..."

"Yes. I know. I was just speaking to her. I know what you have done last night, Anthony. And it's a good thing that you are already suspended or I would have had to suspend you. Drinking on duty, stalking and attacking women. Most shameful behaviour!"

"But sir, that is not what happened. The thing is..."

"I am not interested in hearing your defense. I have called to tell you that though Constable Braganza told me not to take any action against you, I think I should. She doesn't want to press charges against you. You attacked a lady and an active public servant. She told me you had had a break down while on duty and had tried to attack Mrs Krishnan, too! Is that true?"

"Sir, I was... Yes sir," Tony said. He was indeed guilty of that charge and ashamed of it, too.

"I know her personally, and I must say, I am surprised. When she spoke to me about putting you on leave for some time, she never mentioned this attacking incident. Anthony George, if you do not seek medical help from a psychiatrist, I will make sure you are dismissed."

"But sir..."

"No excuses. The only reason I am giving you this chance is because Constable Braganza said you have become mentally imbalanced since your daughter's death. This is my first and last warning, stay away from that lady," he said, indignant, and disconnected the call.

"Shit!" he said in frustration and threw his phone.

Leslie had played him and planned last night's drama so that she could make sure that no one believed Tony when the time came.

He felt a hand on his shoulder after sometime and saw Arvind looking at him enquiringly. Dr Shrinivasan and Eleena were awake too. Tony, exhausted mentally, told them what the commissioner had said and the silence went unbroken for some time. No one knew what to say or do anymore.

"We have to continue to follow her." Tony said sometime later with resolve.

"What!? What for? We know that she is the killer. But the commissioner is not ready to believe you now. I was telling you all along that we should involve the authorities, but you wouldn't listen! Now, Sam's killer is roaming around while we sit here, our heads hanging, like a bunch of losers!" Arvind voice rose.

"We have to follow her because there might be another chance. A chance to catch her red-handed. If she is the serial killer, then she will do it again. She will find a new prey and when she goes after another child, we will be there to catch her!"

"Have you really lost you mind, Tony? That might take days, weeks, months, maybe even years! How are you going to shadow the woman you have been asked to stay away from?"

"He is not alone," Eleena said, a tear rolling down her cheek. "I am with you, Tony. I will help out whenever I can. I know what it's like to lose a child."

"I am with you too, Tony, and I also think it will be a good idea. She has killed more than one victim in one place; and serial killers always follow a set pattern, they also have a trigger usually. We just have to wait it out, and when she tries to harm another child, we will be there to save the girl and catch her red-handed in the process," Dr Shrinivasan said.

After sometime, Uncle Shri asked his nephew. "What other choice do we have, anyway? Sit by and let her kill others?"

"You have all lost your minds! I am not going to waste my time like this. Didn't Pervez Anna say that the DCP is his friend? Call him," he said, infuriated.

Tony called Pervez and told him that he knew Leslie was the killer. Though quicker than the rest to absorb this new update, he gave Tony more bad news.

"Commissioner has asked the DCP to find out everything about you and not just you, about me and Arvind Maran too!"

"*What!?*" Tony said stunned. "*Yes!* I was about to call you from work. This Leslie bitch told the Commissioner that we were encouraging you in stalking her and had illegally dug up her case files. Now the commissioner wants DCP to have a look in the matter. He has told me that he will manage the situation somehow, but this shit has blown out of proportion! How did she know I was helping you!?"

"I don't know, Anna. I never said your name in her presence. I am sorry Pervez, for putting you in this mess."

"Don't be a moron now! I got into this knowing what I was doing. Have you got any concrete evidence that will prove beyond a doubt that she is the killer?"

"No, Anna," Tony said dejected.

"So she has managed to initiate an inquiry against three officers of good standing. And we can't do shit about her because we don't have evidence!? That sucks!" Pervez said, speaking in a fit of rage.

"But why do they think you were stalking her!?" he asked as his thought went back and forth, wondering what to do next. As a father of two, Pervez Sheikh felt most aggravated at the thought that a child molester and killer was on the streets and he couldn't do anything about it.

"Because I attacked her last night and everyone saw it. So now she is saying I am stalking her."

"Oh... then we are screwed." Pervez Sheikh said, knowing that a suspended officer attacking a lady was the worst scenario possible.

When Tony hung up, Arvind was still looking angrily at Tony.

Tony was stalking Leslie and that he was obsessed with her to a point of getting physically violent with her became common knowledge in town.

Tony tried talking to Mrs Krishnan next, and she sympathetically heard everything Tony said. But thinking that he had finally had a breakdown that had pushed him over the edge, she didn't believe anything. Even the Doctor's assessment and Arvind's witness of Leslie's threat to Tony went unheard. A woman and a mother of a girl herself, Mrs Krishnan refused to even consider that a woman, and one like Leslie, could be the perpetrator of such monstrous crimes.

"I will speak to the Commissioner to not take any legal action against you. And I will speak to Leslie to let the matter go, as well. But I can't do more than that. I saw you, Tony, attacking this poor woman. I saw how scared she looked," she said miserably.

"Ma'am, you don't understand. Leslie confessed!"

"How is that possible? I was watching you guys the whole time. I saw how you followed her, how she came behind you to catch you watching her. Then you guys were talking for some time amicably. What happened then that you started arguing with her? She looked scared to death." She paused.

"Anyway, when did she confess to the murders, Tony? When you were trying to choke her or when she was calling out for help?"

"You need help, Tony. You need to see a doctor, and not Arvind's uncle. He sounds delusional as well. Please see a real doctor who will be able to help you," she said, and hung up.

24th November
Thursday

"Tony, are you coming to join the search for Shwetambari or not?" Arvind asked frustrated at the silence on the other end.

"Can you put me in Leslie's team?"

"No. No one will approve of that. And Leslie, we know, will provoke you again. You want a restraining order now? We need to lay low for some time Tony, and this is about Shweta. Mrs Krishnan is out of her mind."

"Okay. But can you be on Leslie's team?"

"Yes, I suppose I can."

"Okay. I will be there in fifteen minutes." Tony said and hung up. Splashing water on his face, he was out of the house in less than five minutes.

Tony, Dr Shrinivasan and Arvind had been staking out Leslie's house since Monday. Angry as Arvind had been, and he was still cross at Tony for having delayed reporting their findings to the commissioner before Leslie did anything, he had continued to help Tony.

They had worked out a system to be able to watch her constantly and it had been successful so far.

Arvind watched her at work and sometimes after work too, if he could get out at the same time as Leslie. Leslie had, so far, once taken a half day leave on Wednesday, and Tony had reached her house immediately, but she had not come home till evening 8.00 p.m.

Dr Shrinivasan helped out whenever he could in watching Leslie and Tony kept an eye on her during the rest of the time, watching her like a hawk.

A couple of times he had felt that maybe Leslie knew she was being followed. Once she had paused at her door and glared at Tony's wife's car; that was on Monday evening. But she hadn't done anything else out of ordinary. She went to the police station at 9.00 a.m., came back around 7.30 p.m. Thomas came around 10.00 p.m., by which time Leslie was usually asleep, judging from the lights in the house.

She had gone out for a run on Tuesday morning at 4.00 a.m. and Tony hadn't been able to keep up with her while maintaining his distance at the same time. He had lost her near the waterfall, a few kms from sunset point. She had come out, almost in his path in the woods, around 5.30 a.m. and ran back home with Tony following behind.

And now Shwetambari Krishnan, a five-year-old, was missing from her own bed. Mrs Krishnan had put her daughter to bed at 10.00 p.m. the night before, she said, and this morning when she went to wake her for school at 6.00 a.m., she was not there.

Tony himself had fallen asleep around 09.00 p.m. when Uncle Shri had taken over. Uncle Shri said she never left her house and he had been awake, alert, till Tony had woken up at 01.00 a.m. She had left for work, in the morning and Tony had followed her till the police station.

But something felt wrong to Tony. He had got a call from Arvind even before he reached the police station that Shweta was missing and a search party was being organized.

The search that began in the morning around 9.00 a.m. on Thursday went on till 01.00 a.m. of Friday.

Almost all the locals of Marsti participated and the school was announced closed, as were local shops and offices. Tony knew this had to have been Leslie. There was no doubt in his head that he had let the tragedy fall on Shwetambari and her life was in peril because he had made some mistake.

Thomas was in Tony's search group and he avoided even walking near Tony. As the search came to an end, while the inconsolable Mrs Krishnan kept crying for her daughter, Tony approached Thomas and smiled at him.

"How are you, Thomas?" he asked politely.

"Don't talk to me!" Thomas said through gritted teeth. "You tried to kill my wife, and now you ask me how I am? I am angry. I am hurt. I thought we were friends. But you are just a crazy motherfucker! Well, at least now everyone knows what a psycho you are!"

"Yes, you are right. And I am seeing a doctor for it. I just wanted to say sorry to you buddy. I really don't know what came over me. I want to apologies to Leslie too, but I am not supposed to be talking to her. Will you tell her I am sorry? Please?" Tony said, remorsefully.

"Oh... Yes... I will tell her you said sorry. Are you really seeing a psychiatrist?" he asked suspiciously, interested in this piece of gossip.

Tony said he was and offered to drop Thomas home, trying to find out anything he could about what Leslie had been up to in the last few days.

"I am sure she must be very scared. The poor thing. I really don't know what I was thinking or what overcame me when I attacked her. Is she okay?"

"Yeah, kind of. Her nausea has started again, but that happens every now and then anyway. She is running more. Every day. But that too is not new. On Monday night, she came back covered in mud! Can you believe it? I saw her clothes in the hamper the next morning, damp and stained. But like I said, nothing is new there. So don't worry. I will talk to her and say you are sorry for what happened," Thomas said putting his hand on Tony's lap.

Tony was too occupied thinking, to notice Thomas's hand caressing his thigh and inching towards his crotch.

"How did I miss Leslie going for a jog on Monday?" he muttered under his breath. He had been watching the house all night, quite alert.

Then a sudden realisation struck. "Thomas, you have a backyard, don't you?"

"Of course! Almost every house in Marsti has a backyard. Why do you ask?" he asked politely, hand snaking up higher on Tony's thigh. Tony halted the car and looked at Thomas, "Would you like me to put your hand in its correct place, Thomas?" Tony asked, his voice calm, but eyes fierce.

"I can walk the rest of the way from here, I think," Thomas said, scared of the madness he had seen in Tony's eyes.

Tony got out of the car once Thomas left and called Arvind to check where Leslie was. "She left some time ago, Tony, said her husband was picking her up. Why?"

"How long ago was this?"

"Ten, maybe fifteen minutes. Why Tony? What has happened now?"

"Come to Sunset Point in the woods. Now! I have one torch in my car. Get yours too. And reach as soon as possible, Arvind."

Tony drove to the closest road from Sunset Point where he had lost Leslie the other day. Arvind was waiting for him when Tony reached. He conveyed the conversation with Thomas to Arvind and they started searching the woods immediately, rushing in opposite directions.

After an hour, Arvind called Tony to ask if they should check David's guesthouse again.

"She won't use the same place again, Arvind. She is too smart to. There has to be another place. Thomas said her clothes were muddy and damp. But it hasn't been raining lately and it didn't rain on Monday for sure! Where could she have gone?"

"Maybe she has dug some underground place to hide the child?"

"Shut up, Arvind! How would two thousand people walking back and forth, miss an underground hide away? And that would have taken too much time anyway."

"Come on, Tony! It is possible. I mean, she has been coming here at nights and you have missed her because she was sneaking out of the back door. We don't know how long she has been at it. Maybe she started planning this kidnapping soon after Sam's. How else could she get muddy if not from digging the ground?" Arvind said, indignant.

"Okay. Call Dr Shrinivasan and Eleena; we will need their help, because if we go by your theory, then this hole she has dug could be anywhere. Ask them to come to Sunset Point."

"Why Sunset Point? I am almost at the waterfall. You should come here, the grounds here is wetter than it is on the cliff."

"That is a good idea, Arvind. She could have hidden the child somewhere there. And if the grounds are wet, then digging would have been easier too. I will be there," Tony said as he started running towards the waterfall.

"Exactly. And I know this place very well... In fact... there is a place behind the waterfall where we as kids used to go with our friends! I will check it out. Come fast," Arvind said and hung up. His phone rang again. It was Tony.

"What is behind the waterfall?" Tony yelled.

"There is a small crammed space where kids usually go to make out. Not many people know about it. I didn't think of that before. I am right here, Tony. I will have a look," Arvind said and hung up before Tony could stop him.

Tony ran, but it took him ten minutes to reach the waterfall. Arvind was nowhere to be seen and he didn't know where exactly the place was. Tony dropped his phone and walked straight towards the waterfall.

Stumbling to the base of the waterfall, using his hands and fingers, he started feeling for the space between the rocks, torch held between his lips and teeth.

Tony came out on the other side of the waterfall, water in his eyes, knees scrapped from stumbling over rocks. He had not felt any space between the rocks. And then he started walking back, this time hands at waist level. And finally he felt a void instead of rocks and almost fell in.

Tony bent to the level of his hands and finally saw the place. It was elevated at about 2 feet from water level, size of 5 ft. by 10 ft., and height of just under 3 ft. And laying on the damp rocky ground was Arvind, unconscious, with blood pooled around his head. He moved the torch and saw Shweta, unconscious, in the far corner, her face scratched, mouth taped, hands and legs tied. Leslie was nowhere to be seen.

Tony bent and was about to crawl inside when something hit him on his head. Turning around, hand on the back of his head, he saw Leslie standing there with a rock in her hand.

Tony, without thinking, half-dazed, pulled back his hand

and punched her across her face. She fell in the knee deep water. His other hand holding the back of his head came away bloody, the excruciating pain making him faint. He bent and crawled a bit and pulled Shwetambari out. He carried her out of the waterfall. Other than a few scratches, the child looked unharmed physically.

Tony went back and pulled Arvind out and shouldered him to where Shwetambari was. He had seen Leslie make a run towards the woods, but he could not leave the child alone and go behind her. He called Eleena from his phone and told her to come to the waterfall with Mrs Krishnan, and to tell her that Shweta was okay, but they needed first-aid for her and Arvind, and back up to catch the killer. Eleena did the same immediately and was out of the house before Tony had hung up.

"Arvind, wake up!" Tony said slapping his face hard.

He finally came to consciousness and sat up in a jerk and then held his spinning head to steady himself. "Tony! Thank god you found us," Arvind said when he saw the unconscious child next to him.

"Arvind, keep an eye out for Leslie. She ran in that direction and I am going to follow her, but she may double back and try to hurt you guys again. Untie the child and take care of her. Tell her everything is fine, and her mother is coming. I have called Eleena, she should be here soon with help. Don't go anywhere unless you have to hide. And if Leslie does come back, please don't try to be a hero. Just hide."

"Yes Tony, she is damn strong, man!" Arvind said, touching his own head and crotch.

Tony ran into the woods to catch his daughter's murderer, to catch the woman who had once been a little girl like his daughter but had grown up to become the tormentor instead of the protector.

Nancy almost tripped running away from her uncle. She was scared of being caught by him. She was scared that he would hurt her again. She continued to run, unconscious of the fact that there was blood flowing from her knees where she had cut herself at the waterfall.

She could hear her uncle catching up, his footsteps close behind her now. Looking back, she stumbled again, but this time her leg got caught in a branch and as she fell, a sharp branch pierced through her calf. In pain, Nancy slumped down, holding her leg. Her uncle was close behind now. She could hear him coming, closer and closer.

The only thought on her mind was that she was lost in the woods, and her uncle would come any moment and catch her. The pain in her body forgotten in her fear of the pain her uncle would cause her, her eyes red, brimmed with tears. She looked around, petrified.

And he had found her, again, after so many years. She could hear his heavy breathing, could smell his sour breath on her face, and could feel his cold hand ripping her jeans' buttons and then being thrust into her, and could feel the pain that was greater than the one in her leg. She yelled out.

Tony heard someone crying out and ran in the direction. He was worried that Leslie may have hurt Arvind and gotten to Shweta. The shrill cries were that of a little child yelping in pain, like his Sam used to in his nightmares.

"Shweta, I am coming. Where are you, child?" he yelled back, running, looking around and finally saw Leslie, crying, and praying, hugging her knees. She was crying out for her mother. Her voice that of a little girl, pain etched in her features. She kept repeating the same thing, pleading first and then yelling out in pain. "Oh God, please help me. I will be a good girl. Please help me god. Ma!" Tony thought this was some ploy, but as he walked closer, cautiously, he saw a piece of wood sticking out of her leg, her bloody hand, and most baffaling was that her jeans pants were undone, almost ripped till her knees.

When Tony touched her shoulder, she yelled piercingly and slumped as if unconscious. Tony took his phone out and was about to dial Eleena's number when another voice issued from Leslie – a rough, harsh voice of a middle-aged man, a voice he had heard at the Town Hall when Leslie had told him that she was the murderer. Tony halted, surprised; there was extreme agony on Leslie's face but the voice held no pain, only malice.

Then, Tony saw something that he hadn't imagined in his worst nightmares. Leslie, whimpering in pain, but talking with a lustful manly voice, started molesting her own body.

"No uncle, please don't uncle," she said in a little child's pleading voice.

"How will I make love to you if I don't, Nancy?" she said in a manly lustful voice.

Disgusted, Tony turned his eyes away, and Leslie cried in pain again. "Ma!"

And her own other hand slapped across her face, muffling her yells as the other hand hurt herself, drawing more blood.

"Ma!" cried Leslie loudly in a voice that Tony couldn't believe was coming from a grown woman.

Unable to help himself, Tony knelt next to Leslie, but didn't know what was happening or what she was doing. Only that this woman was causing herself unbearable pain.

"Touch me Sheena, touch me, and bite me, yes! Like that?"

And the hand held her own breast hard and another yell escaped the mouth of the thirty-year-old, but the voice was again that of the little girl. This voice was different, it sounded younger than the one before. There was a lisp in this voice that hadn't been there a minute back. Tony saw Leslie starting to bite herself, hard enough to draw blood.

Tony bent close to Leslie and touched her forehead. She didn't react to Tony's touch, but continued to bite herself.

"Leslie, please stop. What are you doing?" No response from Leslie.

"Emma, child, you are hurting yourself. Please stop." Still nothing.

"Nancy, sweetheart, please stop hurting yourself." Tony pleaded now, tears in his eyes.

"Help me. Please," she begged looking up at Tony. Not only her voice, but even her features looked like that of a small child. She was helpless, defenseless.

Realization dawned on Tony.

And the feature changed again and the voice that ensued chilled Tony to the bone. "Nancy! Sheena! Jayanta! Seema! Anoska! ....."

The manly voice was counting on his fingers when he stopped suddenly.

"Now I know why uncle used to hurt me. He loved it. He said so. Uncle hurt me because he loved it. Uncle also loved me. Uncle still loves me. He loves me every night. He loves small, beautiful girls. But he doesn't hurt me when he loves other girls. I should let him love other girls. Why won't Paa stop him? Please come... Mom... Paa..!" now the voice shifted to a seemingly adult voice, younger than Leslie, but older than Nancy.

Tony was openly crying now. He felt afraid to touch the woman in front of him.

"Mom, Paa, please come. It really hurts." Nancy started sobbing softly, piteously.

"Stop the crying!" shouted Garry Damascus. "Stop the bloody crying!"

The blade lying next to her, that Tony had just noticed, was picked up and she cut herself across her thigh, moaning in pleasure and crying in pain at the same time.

"Amma!" yelled another child, this one sounding different than the others. The right hand dropped the blade and clamped on Leslie's mouth with force.

Tony was watching the woman raping herself, thinking she was her own uncle!

He tried to hold Leslie. Grasping her left hand by the arm, he pulled the other hand away from her mouth, and Leslie breathed.

"Who the fuck are you?" yelled Garry in an angry voice, suddenly noticing Tony, and the hand Tony was holding started to struggle to break free, while Leslie continued to cry.

He could hear the police sirens now.

Leslie's left hand, slick with blood, slipped out of Tony's, and with a vicious swipe of the paw, she scratched at his neck. Her hand reached for the blade she had dropped on the ground. Tony swiped the blade away and slapped Leslie. He held the other hand again.

"Appa!" the little child called out for help now.

"Mummy!" another loud sob escaped her mouth.

He could hear the footsteps now, running in their direction. Someone shouted out his name and Tony answered back loudly.

The police came, guns at the ready, followed by a limping Arvind, and an out of breath Eleena. Mrs Krishnan stood behind with an unconscious Shweta in her arms, looking petrified. The hospital ambulance siren could be heard too.

They all stood immobile. The scene in front of them was one they wanted to look away from, horrified, but couldn't.

Epilogue

9th January 2018

"Yes doctor, our NGO will take care of all your expenses and stay too. I will personally pick you up from the airport tomorrow and take you to the hospital," Tony said and hung up.

When the cab halted outside Chennai Psychiatric Facility, Tony got out with a bouquet of flowers and three bags.

His phone rang as he was about to enter the old building in front of him. With a smile he picked it up and before he could say 'Hello', a voice yelled into his ears loud enough for him to pull it away.

"Anna, I am going to be a dad!"

"That's Amazing! How is El now?" Tony asked, excited himself at the news.

"She is much better now that she knows she's going to be a mother," he said laughing.

"The doctor said the first trimester is always a little difficult and the nausea and weakness is all part of it. In seven-and-a

-half months, I will be a father!" Arvind yelled. Tony could hear his smile in his words.

"So is she taking a leave or will she be allowed to work?" Tony asked Arvind, but the reply came from Eleena herself.

"Of course I will work, Anna. This is just temporary and I can't take a leave like this. A couple of days' rest and then back to work. Nurses orders!" She said laughing as Arvind started humming a tuneless tune which seemed to get louder and louder.

"You should have seen Arru right now. I think he has lost his mind! He is dancing on the table. Arvind, remove your shoes at least. Or I will make you clean the whole house!" she said and the next voice on the phone was Arvind's.

"Anna, she is right. You should have been here. At your home. With us. Come back now, Anna. You can join duty immediately. Mrs Krishnan was asking for your number again to apologize for not believing you and the commissioner has himself got in touch with you to resume duty. Please come back, Tony."

"I can't, Arvind. Nancy needs me here and there are so many girls who... But I will come for the delivery, and next weekend, I will come and meet you both. We will celebrate. But we go out to eat, please. Last time you cooked, I had stomach ache for two days." he finished with a laugh.

"Tony, you can't change the subject. This NGO thing is not you. You can help far more people by catching the culprits," Arvind said somberly.

"I have to go now. I will let you know when I am coming and give my hug and love to El and the baby. Bye." He hung up before Arvind started trying to convince him again.

The receptionist, a pretty girl with pleasant manners smiled and nodded at Tony as he walked in and an attendant immediately followed him to the first floor and opened the door to a room.

Inside, Leslie sat in a chair by the window, staring at the banyan tree outside, smiling. On the table in front of her lay her drawing book and crayons.

Leslie had been in a stupor for three days after being taken into custody. She had been violent with herself, her mind in a constant flux between her alter egos.

She had to be kept on heavy drugs to control her aggression, but as soon as she would start to gain conscious, she would start struggling against the ties that had held her hands and legs to keep her from running away or hurting herself and others.

Being force fed and constantly on medication, when on the third day she had the most violent of the episodes, even the doctors had thought she wouldn't survive it for long.

Her voice had become hoarse, her hands and legs bruised to the point of the superficial skin being rubbed off and bleeding.

The leg which had been injured in the woods, bleeding profusely, in spite of the bandages being changed three to four times a day, from the muscles being engaged constantly.

She had finally collapsed without the drugs on the third night while a nurse had rushed to get Dr Moore and Dr Shrinivasan.

Tony, who had been heartbroken at finally understanding what the trauma had done to Leslie, had been at the hospital all through, going home only to shower and change.

Every time he thought of his Sam, he wanted to murder the one who had touched her, hurt her. But he hadn't been able to take out his anger on Leslie in the woods or after that. Those three days in the hospital, Tony had wondered if he should have killed her in the woods instead of calling Eleena.

But the way he had found her, he hadn't been able to hurt her; he had felt pity.

He still wondered if he had found the culprit that day, a rapist and murderer, or a victim.

He hadn't been able to decide if she was the culprit or the victim.

When she gained conscious, Tony, Dr Moore and the court appointed psychiatrist had been by her bedside, ready with the sedatives to put her back to sleep.

But the one who woke up was not Leslie.

When Tony entered, she jumped up in joy and hugged him.

"Happy birthday Nancy. Look what I got for you," he said handing her the bags and putting the flowers in a plastic jug on her bedside table.

The room was sparsely decorated, clean, open. There were soft toys on the bed covered in white cotton bed sheets, including a life-size teddy bear that had once belonged to his daughter. Toys littered the floor, along with books and crayons.

"Gifts!" she laughed and took the bags to her bed where she started opening each package. Tony had got her new clothes, new crayons and some colouring books.

"Tony, I made some new paintings. Will you put them on the wall too, please?" she asked looking up. She pulled a few pages, haphazardly torn from her book, from under her pillow and handed it to Tony and went back to admiring her purple dress.

Tony took the drawings and went to the wall that was almost covered in drawing papers. He took out the tape from his pocket and started putting them up.

"Have you spent all your time drawing or have you memorized the poem too?"

"Of course, I have! But when will you teach me the one about 'The Spider and The Fly'?" She asked as she started leafing through the books.

"Who told you about that one?" Tony asked surprised.

In the last six months, since Tony had finally received the court permission to start working with Leslie, she had never mentioned it.

"Huh? I don't know. But I remember some of the lyrics. Will you teach it to me, please?" she asked looking up at him. Her innocent eyes belonged not to the thirty-four-year-old that she was. They were the eyes of the six-year-old Nancy who had not met her monster in Garry Damascus yet.

The doctors thought, in time, she would remember everything and then her chances of going back to being violent were very real. But Tony knew he would try everything in his power to protect her innocence this time.

"This year, we learn other poems. Next year, I will teach you The Spider And The Fly, Okay?"

"Okay." She said smiling and started filling colours in the flowers book.

"Did you have your lunch?"

"No. I was waiting for you. We will eat together."

"Okay honey. What do you want to eat?"

"Cake! It's my birthday!"

"We will have cake in the evening. But what will you have for lunch?" Tony asked sitting on a chair.

"Tony? Did you talk to my ma and paa? When are they coming to get me? I don't like it here."

"Soon baby. And I come to meet you every day. Don't I?"

"Yes. But I want to go home. And I want to meet ma and paa. Why don't they come to see me?" She said in a small voice.

Holding back his own tears, Tony asked her how she liked her new dresses.

"I can take them back if you don't like them." he said, looking seriously at her and pretended to fold them away.

"No! I love them! And especially this one!" she said snatching a salwar kameez from her bed.

"Purple is my favourite colour!"

"Mine too." he said, remembering his daughter's last birthday.

"Now let's get something in your yummy tummy. Shall we?" He said tickling her on her forearm.

Laughing, she said, "I wanna have pancakes!"

Tony laughed. "Pancakes it is then."